"'Hannah, I want you to have half of my farm...'"

"What?" The question exploded out of Ethan as his tilting chair slammed on the floor. "Read that again?"

Dan sighed. "Please, Ethan. Just wait. Let me finish. 'Hannah, you get this half of the farm on one condition. You stay here in Riverbend for six months, and you stay on the farm. When six months is over, you can do what you want with your half. If you leave before the six months are up, you don't get half.'" Dan glanced up at Hannah. "Do you understand what I just read?"

Though Hannah nodded, she struggled to process the concept. She chanced a quick look at the man beside her.

Ethan rocked in his chair as well, his face hard and angry. Not difficult to see he didn't like the idea, either.

Books by Carolyne Aarsen

Love Inspired

*Stealing Home

CAROLYNE AARSEN

and her husband Richard live on a small ranch in northern Alberta, where they have raised four children and numerous foster children, and are still raising cattle. Carolyne crafts her stories in her office with a large west-facing window, through which she can watch the changing seasons while struggling to make her words obey.

Finally a Family
Carolyne Aarsen

Steeple Hill®

Published by Steeple Hill Books™

STEEPLE HILL BOOKS

Steeple Hill®

ISBN-13: 978-0-373-81364-3
ISBN-10: 0-373-81364-3

FINALLY A FAMILY

Printed in U.S.A.

Accept one another then, just as Christ accepted
you, in order to bring praise to God.
—*Romans* 15:7

To the children who never had a choice.

Chapter One

So this was the town Sam had scurried back to thirteen years ago.

Hannah rocked back and forth on her feet as she looked up and down the main street of Riverbend, studying it through the eyes of one left behind for this place.

The downtown boasted older-style brick buildings and ash trees lining the street, the first hint of spring in the fresh green misting their bare branches. Pleasant enough.

Even though Sam wasn't Hannah's biological father, she thought his nine-year relationship with her and her mother would have given him some permanent stake in their lives. But this town and his extended family had obviously exerted a pull stronger than they had because in the thirteen years he was gone he never came back for her, or wrote or even phoned. Two days ago, however, Hannah received the news from someone named Dan that Sam had passed away three weeks earlier. Dan had politely requested that she come to Riverbend for the reading of Sam's will.

Hannah glanced down Main Street and pulled a face. This town was too small for this big-city girl's liking. Far removed from any major centre and with too many pickup trucks, Hannah thought, her attention drawn by a particularly loud red one making its way down the street toward her.

Hannah flipped open her cell phone and, though she'd had it on since she left Toronto, she checked her messages again. Nothing from Lizzie, her business partner, about how things were progressing on the purchase. Hannah had been reluctant to leave, but Lizzie had encouraged her, saying that nothing was going to happen in the next week, so here she was. She didn't need to meet with the Westervelds till tomorrow, but curiosity had her come a day early. Just to explore and familiarize herself with Sam's surroundings.

Hannah pushed back her own concerns as she drew in a long, slow breath, catching the tantalizing whiff of coffee blended with the distinctive scent of yeast and bread.

She rolled her stiff shoulders as the light changed, already anticipating the bite of the dark brew combined with a warm muffin. Or maybe a Danish.

A couple of young girls slipped past her and dashed across the street, waving at the driver of the noisy red pickup who had turned onto the main street and was parking in front of the bakery.

Then one of the girls bumped into a little boy coming out of the bakery.

The boy dropped his doughnut and his lip quivered as he looked at the treat now lying frosting-side down on the sidewalk. She hurried to his side and knelt in front of him. "Are you okay?" she asked.

He only nodded as she checked her pockets for loose change, but all that came up were a few nickels.

"Susie Corbett, get back here." A man stepping out of the fancy red truck called out to the delinquent girls.

The shorter girl with the curly blond hair heeded the summons and slowed her steps. The other kept running.

"I said now, Susie." While he barked out his demand, the man walked over to Hannah and the little boy.

"You okay, Todd?" he asked, though his gaze came to rest on Hannah.

His eyes, an unusual color of sage, fringed with thick, dark eyelashes, caught and held her attention. His finely shaped lips curved into a crooked smile emphasizing his hollow cheekbones. His expression clearly had one intention. "Thanks for helping," he said, the timbre of his voice lowering and, in spite of knowing what he was playing at, Hannah felt a lift of attraction.

"Back at you." She kept her smile aloof. No sense encouraging one of the locals on a quick visit.

She forced her attention back to the little boy. "Sorry, I don't have enough change for another doughnut," she said.

He sighed and nodded.

"That's okay. Susie will pay," the man said as the girl came nearer. "Won't you, Susie? I think you owe Todd about fifty cents."

"Uncle Ethan," she wailed, but even as she protested, she dug in her pocket. "You won't tell Mom, will you?" she asked as she handed the money over.

"Of course I won't tell your mom, you little twerp. Just don't act like such a toughie." He made the letter *V* with his fingers and pointed them at his eyes. "Remember, I see everything."

Susie gave a nervous laugh.

"Okay, Uncle Ethan." She took a few hesitant steps backward. "Can I go now?"

Uncle Ethan flipped his hand toward her in a dismissive gesture. "Shoo. Run along." Ethan handed the coins to the little boy, who took them with a quickly murmured thank-you and scooted inside the bakery.

When Hannah stood, Ethan looked at her again. This time she caught a hint of puzzlement in his eyes.

"Do I know you?"

Hannah laughed then. Any number of smart remarks came to mind, but his laugh answered hers before she could share any of them.

"That was as lame as a two-legged cat. Sorry." He scratched his head, rearranging his hair.

Weekend cowboy, Hannah deduced, taking in the long legs clad in crisp blue jeans and the polished cowboy boots.

"It's so hard to come up with original lines these days. All the best ones have been taken," Hannah said.

He looked as if he was about to answer with a smart remark of his own when a woman's voice caught his attention.

"Ethan. Wait up." A lithe blond woman came alongside him and slipped her arm through his. "I didn't know *you* were coming to town, handsome."

Ethan flicked his attention toward the woman, then back to Hannah.

Who, officially, was no longer interested. She had spent too much time with guys like Ethan. They encouraged women until things got too serious, then the men developed a sudden severe case of attention deficit disorder and moved on to another woman.

Case in point, Alex Deerborn.

No thanks.

She moved past him, the scent of coffee growing stronger and more tantalizing by the minute.

"So who was that?" she heard the blonde ask.

"I'm not sure, Jocelyn," he responded.

His vague comment made her look back again. "Uncle Ethan" stared at her, a frown pulling his well-shaped eyebrows together, ignoring the woman clinging to his arm.

"I think I saw her."

Morris Westerveld lowered his newspaper and favored his son with a puzzled look. "Saw who?"

"Hannah Kristoferson." Ethan dropped onto the couch in his parents' house, balancing the plate he'd stacked high with the freshly baked peanut-butter-chip cookies he'd found cooling on the kitchen counter. He'd lived on the farm for the past few years, but he still dropped in on his parents in town from time to time. Though his father, the principal of Riverbend High School, hadn't done any work on the farm since he was in high school himself, Ethan often used him as a sounding board. Although his dad had never liked farm work or living on the farm, he humored Ethan by listening.

"Where did you see her?"

"I *thought* I saw her by the bakery after I gave Susie trouble for knocking Todd over."

"What does she look like?"

"She should comb her hair. I'm sure Janie didn't let her out of the house looking like that."

"I meant that Hannah girl."

Ethan took another bite. He had known whom his father meant. He didn't want to think about Hannah and why exactly his uncle Sam had been so insistent she come for a simple reading of a will that had been postponed against her arrival.

"She's tall. Long brownish hair, pretty thick. Curly. She was wearing some kind of bandanna over it. Brown eyes. Doesn't look much different from the picture Uncle Sam had in the house." Ethan added a shrug to the monologue as if to show his father that Hannah was simply an inconvenient blip on his radar instead of someone he'd been wondering about ever since he had first seen that picture.

Ethan didn't want to think about the implications of Hannah's presence and the questions that raised. He preferred to concentrate on the chewy cookies and the shred of comfort they gave him. A feeling in short supply since Sam's death.

Though Sam had been in the hospital for the past six months, each morning Ethan got up, he still expected to see his beloved uncle and farming partner standing by the stove, asking Ethan how he wanted his eggs. Each morning the pain was as deep as the day before. That had made it difficult to get the equipment ready this spring for a job that, of all the farm work, Sam had loved the most. Working the fields.

"She doesn't sound too remarkable," his father said.

"Nope." Ethan took another healthy bite. "Nothing remarkable about her at all."

And he was lying through the peanut butter chips filling his mouth. When he had seen the girl he assumed was Hannah standing on the street corner, her expression holding the faintest glint of humor, he'd been intrigued enough to slow his truck down for a second look.

When she had tried to help out his nephew, she struck a chord in his heart. And then he'd tossed out that lame question.

Do I know you?

He blamed his lapse on the hint of laughter in the shape of her arching eyebrows and her soft mouth. Brown hair flowing like melted chocolate over her shoulders and down her back had also added to his momentary brainlessness.

In spite of his rather uncharacteristically gauche question, he still wanted to go after her and ask her a few questions, which would have violated his hard-won rules for living.

Keep your pride. Don't go running after any girl. Let them come to you.

This had been his mantra ever since Colby left

him the day before their wedding because she suddenly decided she couldn't move onto the farm.

It took him four months to get over her, five months to use up all the envelopes that came with the thank-you cards and six months to decide he would never go running after a girl again.

"Hannah was supposed to be here by today, so that girl could easily have been her." Morris Westerveld gave his newspaper a shake and dived into the news of the world again.

Ethan sighed and picked a crumb off his fingertip.

If that girl was Hannah, she would bring nothing but questions and potential trouble to the family and—more specifically—to him.

The family had all breathed a collective sigh of relief when Sam came back from Ontario thirteen years ago. Grandpa Westerveld, Sam's partner on the family farm, had been injured in a bad accident and Sam was needed. Ethan was sixteen at the time and chafing to quit school so he could work full-time with his grandfather on their family farm. Ever since he could throw a bale, Ethan had spent evenings and weekends and every holiday helping his grandpa.

Sam slipped back into the groove but never said much about the nine years he'd been gone or the woman that he'd been living with and her little girl. Nor did he ever get married.

After Grandpa Westerveld died, Sam, his son, took over the struggling farm, and when Ethan graduated from high school Sam took his nephew on as his new partner.

Now Sam was dead, after a six-month battle with cancer. And, per Sam's request, Sam wanted one Hannah Kristoferson and Ethan Westerveld at a private reading of his will, the reading to be put off until such time as one Hannah Kristoferson could be tracked down.

Though no one understood the reasons for Sam's unusual request, the Westerveld family all knew about Hannah and her mother, Marla, and their involvement with their brother and uncle.

Sam and his father had had a falling out and Sam had left, determined to make it on his own. He started hitchhiking across Canada and got as far as Toronto, where he met Marla and Hannah at a Laundromat. Hannah was three. He dated Marla for a time and then moved in.

During Sam's stay in Toronto, the family kept up a regular communication with Sam. They all wrote and phoned. When he returned, he never mentioned Marla or Hannah. The only reminder of those lost years was a few pictures and some homemade cards, and the cheques he sent Marla Kristoferson every month.

When Sam was admitted to the hospital, he asked the family to try to find Hannah so he could see her before he died. By the time they finally found her, Sam had been dead and buried for three weeks.

Ethan pushed himself off the couch. He didn't need to give Hannah or her mother any more headspace. He had too much work to do and too little time to do it in.

Chapter Two

Hannah paused at the entrance to the acreage to check the name on the sign: Dan and Tilly Westerveld. She put the car in gear, took a calming breath and turned down the driveway. The tall spruce trees lining the driveway could have been welcoming or sinister, depending on one's mental state.

Right now, echoes of Hansel and Gretel were teasing her memories. Though Hannah was pretty sure no tempting gingerbread house complete with wicked witch lay at the end of the graveled driveway, a sense of foreboding still surrounded her as she drove.

The driveway gave one more turn and then opened up into a large open space, also surrounded by spruce trees. She slowed, then turned toward an area she presumed was a parking lot. It was occupied by a small white car and the same bright red truck Hannah had seen her first day in town.

Hannah locked the car and, as she slipped the keys into her purse, took a moment to look at the Westerveld home. The house was large, all shades of cream and brown, and set off by a heavy field-stone foundation.

Contemporary, imposing and probably expensive.

The house had two wings connected by a thirty-foot-high section composed of glass, creating an abundance of natural light.

Dan Westerveld must share Sam's love of gardening, from the look of the large landscaped lawn broken up with clumps of shrubs and flowers. Beyond the house Hannah caught a glimpse of a fountain and a gazebo flanked by flower beds.

Spikes and a few patches of green broke through the dirt. She would love to see this place in the summertime, she thought with a tinge of disloyalty, letting the peace and quiet of the place surround her.

It had taken a lot of money and a lot of time to make this place look like this. The house alone would have set them back beaucoup bucks, never mind the landscaping costs.

What was a simple hairdresser with plans of buying an old, decrepit salon thinking this family owed her?

Her anger and her grief over Sam were inextricably intertwined with her anger against his family. If they hadn't interfered, she might have had a father yet. If the Westervelds had stayed out of their business, her teen years might have had some cohesion and order instead of the chaos and confusion it fell into after Sam left.

She strode up the brick walk, marched up the slate steps to the recessed front door and pressed the doorbell.

Hannah, taking charge.

After a few moments, the door opened to reveal a middle-aged woman clad in blue jeans, a corduroy blazer over a white T-shirt and a polite smile.

"You must be Hannah. Come in." She stood aside to let Hannah in. "I'm Tilly Westerveld. Welcome to our home."

The interior was even more impressive than the exterior. The entrance soared two floors, lit by the wall of windows.

"Can I take your coat?" Tilly asked as Hannah's eyes were drawn, against their will, to a staircase arching gracefully up to the second floor. To her right, through a set of sliding wooden and glass doors, she saw upholstered chairs pushed up to a gleaming wooden table in a dining room, also open to the second floor.

"Sure," Hannah said, feeling a bit dazed by her surroundings.

"Dan and Ethan are in the study. Would you like a cup of coffee or tea before you go in?"

"Um…no, thanks." She gave Tilly a belated smile.

"Would you like me to show you the way?"

Tilly's own smile was as polite as before but Hannah caught a hint of tightness around her mouth. She guessed Tilly Westerveld wasn't elated to see her.

"That's not necessary. Just tell me how to get there."

"The study is just past the stairs. Turn to your left and then left again. The door is open." Tilly waved her hand toward the hallway leading off the foyer.

"Thanks." Feeling vulnerable without her jacket, Hannah folded her arms over her stomach and followed Tilly's directions, a sense of unreality surrounding her like a cloud. She tried not to stare as a double set of glass doors off the hallway to her right afforded her a glimpse of another large room, the great room, she suspected, with its massive fireplace, numerous leather chairs and couches and floor-to-ceiling windows overlooking the backyard. A woman sat curled up in one corner of the couch. She looked up as Hannah passed and lowered her book, her features transforming from curiosity to bored disinterest.

Hannah heard the sound of murmuring voices and made another turn, focusing on the reason she was here. The door to the study was half-open, so Hannah knocked lightly on it and waited.

"Hannah Kristoferson?"

The door opened and a man stood in front of her, tall, slightly graying hair, friendly blue eyes with laugh lines radiating from their corners. Just like Sam's. His genuine smile created a hitch in her heart which, compounded with the embarrassment of being caught snooping, made her feel flustered.

"Yes. Sorry. Your wife…told me to come here—" she waved backward, down the hallway in the general direction of the rest of the house "—so I…I'm here. I didn't mean to stare. It's just…your yard. It's…it's lovely."

And…stop.

"Why, thank you, Hannah." Dan Westerveld walked toward the window and beckoned for her to follow. "Come here and you can have a better look."

"No, that's okay. I mean, I'm here for a meeting, right?"

"Don't fuss on account of me," she heard a deep voice drawl from the other side of the room.

A tall figure stood in front of a set of book-shelves covering the entire wall, floor to ceiling. He held a magazine in one hand, and continued flipping through it while he watched her.

His faint smile mocked her even as she read the interest in his eyes.

"Uncle Ethan." Ethan *Westerveld*.

Well, she wasn't reciprocating his interest. Coming to this Westerveld stronghold had never been a goal. Cozying up to one of "them," certainly not on the list, no matter how good-looking he may be.

Besides, his whole posture, that look on his face, the smile bordering on self-confident smirk all added up to consummate flirt. Shades of Alex.

She turned back to Dan Westerveld, determined to regain some kind of ground. "Looks to me like you've got peonies coming up in the front. What kind are they?" she asked, making conversation as she walked to the window, allowing herself a good look at the yard she had so admired.

"They come from hearty prairie stock my mother's mother planted on their home site." Dan stood beside her, his hands in the pockets of his pants. "Sam gave me some cuttings a few years back. He farms…farmed, the old place." Dan laughed lightly. "Have to get used to the idea," he said softly. "He was a good man, my brother."

"I'd like to tell you again I'm sorry," Hannah said. Politeness deemed she show some respect for his loss. She wished she could be a bit more sincere, but there it was.

"He had a rough few months, toward the end. He was in a lot of pain, but he died knowing he was a child of God and that he was going on to a better place."

Hannah acknowledged the sentiments with an impersonal nod. She should have known she would bump against Sam's presence and the beliefs of his family often and in many guises. She might as well get used to the pious talk.

"Have you met my nephew Ethan?" Dan asked, walking around to the other side of his desk. "Ethan, this is Hannah Kristoferson. Hannah, Ethan Westerveld."

"We met," Ethan said, laying the magazine aside on a table and sauntering over. A man in charge of his world and comfortable in this place.

"If you want to call that a meeting," Hannah countered, annoyed with his attitude.

Ethan didn't stop until he stood in front of her. "Of course it was." His eyes flicked over her face, as if taking her up on her challenge.

Hannah caught a glint of humor in his gray-green eyes, but she refused to respond.

"Now that you are both here, we can begin." Dan picked up a pair of glasses and slipped them on his face as he moved some papers on his desk aside. Without looking up, he motioned to the two empty chairs in front of the desk. "You two can sit down instead of circling each other like a couple of banty roosters."

"Only one rooster, Uncle Dan," Ethan corrected, hooking the other chair with his shiny cowboy boot and pulling it closer. "And one hen."

"That could be insulting," Hannah said.

"Just trying to be biologically correct," Ethan returned.

"The term is politically correct."

"Honey, when it comes to chickens the only politics is, the male rules the roost."

"Until he gets henpecked."

"Can we start?" Dan prompted, shooting his nephew a warning glance.

Ethan sat, resting his one booted foot across his knee, pushing the chair on its back two legs. Obviously the man felt at home.

Dan gave her a thoughtful look. "Before we start, however, I also want to extend my condolences on the death of your mother."

His sympathies, though kind, caught her off guard. Though it had been only four months since she'd stood alone beside her mother's grave, the sharpest edges of her sorrow had already been dulled.

"I'm sure you must miss her," Dan continued.

"I do, though we hadn't seen much of each other the past few years."

Ethan looked puzzled. "But I thought—"

"I had assumed as much." Dan cut Ethan off. "It had taken us some time to find where she had lived." He uncovered a large envelope, which he placed on the desk in front of him, and folded his hands over the top.

"I feel I should make some kind of formal announcement. While this isn't classified as an official reading of the will, Sam did ask that I read this bequest in this fashion." Dan waited a moment, then picked up the envelope. "I have to warn both of you that I already know what this envelope contains. As executor of Sam's will, I perused every item relating to his estate, including the letter accompanying the will." He paused, his attention resting on Ethan. "I want you both to understand that the contents of the document I'm about to read to you are known only to Sam's lawyer and me."

Ethan nodded and Dan's eyes went to Hannah. She didn't know what was required of her, so she nodded, as well.

Dan gave her a gentle smile and Hannah's curiosity grew.

What was in the envelope that necessitated her flying across the country to attend this meeting?

Dan opened the envelope and pulled out some papers.

"I'll read Sam's letter first." He cleared his throat and began. "'Dear Hannah. I'm going to start with you, because if you are here, you have come the farthest and probably have the most questions....'"

Hannah wrapped her arms across her chest, bracing herself as Dan's even voice read Sam's words, an eerie echo from the grave.

"'...I'm sorry I never phoned you or explained why I left. I wanted to, but that's all I'm going to say about that. I didn't do right by you. I have had tons of time to sit and think and I keep thinking of how I just left you and your mom. So, this is a way to fix that mistake. Dan, I hope you can get hold of her and find her. And, Ethan, please, just be patient.'"

"What does he mean by that?" Ethan said.

"You'll see," Dan said without looking at his nephew. He took a careful sip of water from a glass sitting at his elbow, as if preparing for what he had to say. He read on.

"'I thought a lot about what I'm going to tell you. I didn't make this decision quick or easy. But this is the right thing to do. Hannah, I want you to have half of my farm...'"

"What?" The question exploded out of Ethan as his tilting chair slammed on the floor. "Read that again?"

Dan adjusted his glasses and sighed. This time he held his nephew's angry gaze. "Please, Ethan. Just wait. This is difficult for me, as well, but please let me finish."

Ethan glared at Dan, then leaned back in his chair and crossed his arms over his chest. Hannah tried to ignore his hostile body language as she collected her own confused thoughts. Half of a farm? What could that mean?

Dan pinched his nose, blew out his breath, and continued. "'Hannah, this is all I can give you, to be fair to Ethan. But you get this half of the farm on one condition. You stay here in Riverbend for six months, and you stay on the farm. When six months is over, you can do what you want with your half. If you leave before the six months are up, you don't get half.'" Dan glanced up at Hannah. "Do you understand what I just read?"

Though Hannah nodded, she struggled to process the concept. Half of some farm? If she stayed six months? In what twisted corner of Sam's mind did he think he was doing her any favor with this?

Hannah's salon plans didn't include a six-month detour in this forgotten corner of the world with people who wouldn't acknowledge her presence in Sam's life.

She chanced a quick look at the man beside her.

Ethan rocked in his chair, as well, his mouth set in hard lines, his face angry. Not difficult to see he didn't like the idea, either.

Well, no worries there, Hannah thought, rubbing her forehead. She had only come to Riverbend because of Dan's phone call and Lizzie thinking Hannah had something coming to her from Sam.

And it appeared she had. Half of a farm. She wondered what Lizzie would say to that.

"There is more," Dan said. "He says, 'Hannah,

if you don't want to stay, you lose your half of the farm. I know this comes out of the blue, but I've had time to think while I'm lying here in this hospital. I know I'm dying and I want to fix what I should have fixed long ago. Hannah, I'm sorry. Forgive me. I want to make things right. If you stay, in six months Dan will have another meeting with you. I want you to know I thought of you lots and always loved you.' And that's the end of what he has to say to you." Dan paused a moment as if to give Hannah a chance to absorb the words.

Hannah knew it was going to take more than a few moments to get this all straight in her mind.

Dan glanced at his nephew. "Sam had something to say to you, as well."

"I'm sure he did," Ethan said, his voice a growl.

"I'll read that now. 'Ethan, I hope you understand that I had to do this. I'm sorry for you, as well. You were always going to get the farm like I promised and if Hannah leaves, it's all yours. You've been a big help to me. I couldn't have run the farm without you. You are the only Westerveld who loved the farm like your grandfather did. I want you to know I love you. I'm sorry if this doesn't seem fair to you, but I want you to know I have to do right by Hannah. Because I didn't years ago. You've been a great partner and you're a wonderful and loving nephew. I hope you understand. With love, Sam.'" In the ensuing silence, Dan looked at the letter he still held in his hand, as if trying to digest this information once again. Then he slowly folded it up and inserted it back in the envelope. "And that ends the letter."

Ethan got up, walked to the bookshelf, then turned to his uncle. "I'm trying to understand this, Dan, but I can't. Grandpa Westerveld was working me into the farm. Then, when Sam finally came back, I started working with him. I've put years of my life into that place. I put money into it—" He stopped there, glanced at Hannah, then continued. "Uncle Sam showed me a copy of his will in the hospital. It never said anything about this."

Hannah felt a moment's compassion at the hurt she heard under Ethan's bluster.

"And now, out of the blue he's giving half to…to—" he waved his hand toward Hannah as if she were some piece of detritus clinging to his shiny boots "—her."

"Sam changed the will just before he died. And her name is Hannah," Dan chided.

Ethan ignored Dan's reprimand and leaned back against the shelves. "And what am I supposed to do with a partner who knows zip about farming? Who probably doesn't even know what that place is worth? What was Uncle Sam thinking?"

Ethan's anger battered at Hannah's fragile self-control, his words mixing and churning in her own mind. But curiously his anger at what Sam had done created the opposite effect.

Why didn't he think she deserved half of this farm? Sam had been her "father" for nine years. And after he left them, neither she nor her mother had ever received a dime from him.

Hannah recalled the humiliation of those years post-Sam. Constantly short of money, living with a mother who, after her nervous breakdown, couldn't work. In spite of that, and with the help of the occasional trip to the food bank, she managed to keep a home.

"When did that first will change? And why?" Ethan's expression hardened. "I'm going to contest this. I'll be talking to Jace tomorrow."

Dan leaned back in his chair. "We're not discussing this in front of Hannah," he said quietly. "Suffice it to say this letter was witnessed and notarized and at the time of writing Sam was declared in his right mind. The official will states exactly what I just read, but Sam wrote this letter to explain what he called 'the dry lawyer language' in the will."

"What if I don't want the farm?" Hannah asked.

Dan looked toward her, as if remembering she was there. "Then you don't get anything, I'm afraid."

Hannah tapped her thumbs together, remembering her and her mother's life with Sam. She didn't have anything from Sam now other than memories. This family had everything.

She had no right to the farm, and yet to walk away with empty hands from a family who didn't even acknowledge their presence in Sam's life…

Memories piled upon memories. Whispered telephone conversations Sam had with family members back here. The way he retreated from her and her mother afterward.

Hannah looked down, her emotions coloring her thoughts.

"I don't know what to do," she said.

"Of course not," Dan said, his soft voice sounding as if he understood. "You should give yourself some time to think about this."

"Uncle Dan…"

Dan held up his hand, forestalling any more comments from his nephew.

"I'm sorry," Ethan said. "I've been out of line. It's just…Sam…" His voice broke. Then he strode past the desk to the window and braced one hand on the frame, the other on his hip as he stared out into the yard. He stood in profile to Hannah and for a moment she saw a flash of genuine sorrow on his face.

In spite of his previous antagonism, she found herself feeling bad for him. He had just lost an uncle he'd worked with side by side for so many years. And then to hear this same uncle, out of the blue, had promised a complete stranger half of the farm—well, if she'd just had a shock, she was sure he'd had a bigger one.

"I don't want you to make this decision lightly," Dan said, holding Hannah's regard. "I would really like it if you would come with me to the farm and have a look at Sam's place."

For the briefest moment she felt a tug of emotion. That was silly. She was a city girl. That wasn't going to change.

She had her plans. When the salon she and Lizzie were buying generated enough money, maybe then she could look at a place with a real yard. But for now, she had to be satisfied with what she could realistically afford.

"I thought you might like to at least see where Sam lived before you make your decision," Dan continued. "He took over the farm from our parents. He grew up there, as did we." The wistfulness in Dan's voice landed a gentle hook in Hannah's heart. Roots. Stability. Something she and her mother had never really had.

"I'm sure it's lovely…." She couldn't think of a proper rebuttal, so she just let the sentence hang between them.

Dan scratched his temple with one finger, then sighed. "I would like you to think about this. Sleep on it." He gave Hannah a careful smile. "In fact, I'm not going to listen to any decision today."

"Okay," she said reluctantly. "I'll wait."

Dan smiled. "I'll be praying you make the right choice."

When she was younger, Sam would pray with her. Over time, that eased off. She missed it.

Hannah ducked her head to hide the sudden prickling in her eyes. *Dear Sam, now your brother is praying for me, too.* The thought gave her a peculiar warmth and comfort.

She waited until the thickness in her throat eased, as the silence in the office created its own urgency. She picked up her purse and stood. "So, I guess that's all you need for now?"

"For now," Dan repeated. "When you decide what you want to do, I want you to call me and we'll take things from there."

"I'll call you tomorrow." She slipped her purse over her shoulder.

"When does your flight leave?"

"Sunday evening."

"Then why don't you meet me after church on Sunday. Just to give yourself enough time." He rested his fingertips on Sam's letter.

"Okay. Sunday morning after church, I'll tell you what I decide."

"Do you have a cell phone? Maybe you could give me your number. Just in case." Dan handed her a pen and a piece of paper. She bent over and scribbled the number down. As she straightened, she chanced another look at Ethan at the same time he turned to face her. He was attractive, she conceded.

But that wasn't enough to induce her to live out here for half a year. Not near enough.

"It was a pleasure meeting you," Dan said, holding out his hand across the desk.

Her mother had always told her that Sam's family didn't care for them, so she doubted the sincerity of his comment, but she gave him a polite smile and shook his hand.

"Goodbye, Hannah," Ethan said, turning away from the window. "Thanks for coming."

And she doubted his thanks, too.

"It was nice meeting you." While they were exchanging pleasantries, she figured she might as well add a few of her own. "Again, I'm sorry for your loss. Sam must have meant a lot to both of you, as well." She felt a sudden need to explain. "I need you to know, this is as much of a shock for me as it was for you."

"I understand," Ethan said quietly, though his tight expression told her otherwise. "Thanks for coming." He reached out to shake her hand. She hesitated, then took it.

His rough and callused palm was a surprising contrast to the pressed khaki pants and golf shirt he wore. His eyes held hers as she shook his hand and a frisson of awareness flickered within her.

She pulled her hand away. Definitely time to go.

She gave Ethan a smile, then walked out of the room.

Chapter Three

"So no money? Just half a farm?" Lizzie sounded frustrated, as if hoping Hannah had called to tell her the cash amount of her supposed inheritance. "And what are you going to do with that?"

"I don't know. Sell it, I guess." Hannah let go of the steering wheel of her rental car, down-shifted, grabbed the wheel again and turned her car into the parking lot of the motel.

"In six months."

"I know. I don't know what to do."

"You can't negotiate?"

"With a dead man? Lizzie, this was written out by Sam, signed and sealed in front of a lawyer. I guess this trip was a waste of money."

"I really thought you'd get money up front. Too bad you didn't take up the family on their offer to pay for your ticket."

"I don't want a penny from them...."

"But if you get half of that farm, you'll get more than a penny."

"In six months? I'm not interested."

Hannah pulled into the parking stall in front of her motel room. "So, did you go to the bank?"

"No. Not yet."

Hannah continued as she got out of the car. "I thought you were meeting with them this afternoon?"

"I had to cover your appointments, honey."

Lizzie sounded funny. "Is everything okay yet?"

"Everything's fine. I'm waiting for a call from our loan officer and I'm telling Taylor tonight about the change in our appointment."

"You sure this is still a go?" Hannah got out of the car and walked to the edge of a field bordering the motel. A few shoots of green worked themselves through the tangle of weeds covering the field.

"Absolutely. So when you coming back?" Lizzie asked, abruptly shifting the conversation to another topic.

"Dan Westerveld wanted me to take some time to think about my decision. I'll talk to him on Sunday."

"Excellent idea. Take your time, Hannah. You could use a break. You've been working day and night on that stupid business plan. You've already paid for your ticket. You may as well enjoy some time off work."

"Not my idea of a holiday," Hannah said, lifting her face to the warm spring sun. "Did you talk to the landlord about that leaky tap?"

"He says he'll get to it when he gets to it." Lizzie hummed a little tune and Hannah braced herself.

"What's up, Lizzie?" she asked.

"What do you mean?"

"You're humming. Every time you hum, you've got some confession to make."

Lizzie sighed. "Well, I was going to wait until you were back. I knew once we start running the salon, you'll have more money and you'll probably enjoy being on your own. The apartment won't cost much 'cause it's part of the salon...."

Hannah's heart sank while Lizzie continued.

"And Pete's been making noises about us getting more serious."

"Don't tell me he wants you to move in with him," Hannah said.

"Now don't even start on your old-lady fussing and moralizing," Lizzie continued. "We're going to get married once you and me get the salon going."

"You sound like my mother." Hannah couldn't keep the slightly bitter tone out of her voice. "I'm guessing you're moving out tonight?"

"Yeah."

"I'm disappointed Pete thinks you're that easy, Lizzie." And no sooner had the words left her mouth than Hannah wished she could take them back.

"Not all of us are willing to keep guys at arm's length just because we don't trust them," Lizzie snapped. "You haven't gone out with anyone since Alex dumped you."

"I'll date when I find a guy worth dating." Unlike my mother who, after Sam, went out with any man that smiled at her longer than two seconds.

"And you won't find a guy worth dating if you don't date."

Hannah checked her next comment. She needed Lizzie and didn't dare push her too far. "So you'll be moved out when I'm back." Hannah deliberately pitched her voice low and forced a smile to her face.

"Pete's a good guy, Hannah. He's solid."

Not solid enough to want to marry her.

"Anyway, I gotta go. Gotta make a few more calls about this business...." Lizzie let the sentence hang and Hannah felt a niggle of doubt creep into her mind.

"You sure everything's okay, Lizzie?"

"Yeah. Hey, whaddya think about Pete coming in on this deal? He's got a few dollars he can put in. Will help us out a lot."

"I don't think it's a good idea." She decided to forgo the obvious complications of bringing in a partner who knew precious little about the salon business, never mind the fact that if Lizzie and Pete broke up, the business would be affected.

"I kinda thought you would say that." Lizzie sighed. "Okay. Gotta go. Take care."

Hannah said goodbye, flipped her phone shut and slipped it into her pocket. Lizzie sounded distracted. The whole business deal was taking more out of both of them than Hannah wanted to admit.

She glanced at her watch. Lots of time left in this day. Maybe she should go for a drive and get her mind off all the events bombarding her mind the past few days.

Fifteen minutes later she was heading out of town, down the highway. The only other vehicle was a bright red truck and he had his signal light on for the next exit.

Ethan Westerveld, she realized as she came closer. The truck turned onto a gravel road marked with a hand-painted sign announcing a farm for sale. Was Sam's farm at the end of the road? And what did it look like, this place Sam wanted to split between her and his nephew?

Dan's comment slipped to the forefront of her mind.

Was she sure she didn't want to see the place where Sam grew up?

A niggling curiosity had her putting one foot on the clutch, the other on the brake and her hand on the signal light.

What if he's not going to the farm?

She had little else to do today. She geared down

and turned onto the gravel road, following the dust from Ethan's truck.

She passed a dairy farm and a few other yards. Some neat, some messy. Some of the houses were newer, some old. She passed an abandoned farm site, the graying timbers of the house sagging sadly toward the earth as if missing its previous owners.

And space and space and more space.

She came to the next crossroad and slowed down. A faint cloud of dust hung over the road going left. South of the road, she thought she saw a yard. She caught the glimpse of a house roof tucked against a clump of trees and beyond that, a hip roof barn painted green.

And parked by the barn, a red pickup truck. Ethan's truck.

Hannah put the car in gear, spun the wheel and almost popped the clutch as she gunned the car around the corner, stilling the second thoughts spinning through her head as her tires spun on the gravel.

The sign at the end of the driveway, an exact replica of the one at the entrance to Dan and Tilly's place, assured her that this indeed was Sam's place.

Doubts immediately assailed Hannah. What was she doing here? She had no intention of sticking around; why check the place out?

But Sam had come from and had returned to this place. Why not discover more about the place the man she once loved had spent much of his life? Why not find out what she was turning down, just so she'd know for sure she had made the right decision?

Sam's place had the same treed driveway. But as she came closer to the house, her heart lightened.

Where Dan and Tilly's house clearly said no money had been spared, this place created an entirely different ambience.

The house was a simple cottage style, with a covered veranda, two bay windows flanking a main door. Above the veranda, two dormer windows broke the steeply pitched roof. The house was perched on a hill and, behind and below it, Hannah caught the glint of sunshine bouncing off a small lake.

The place was like a tiny jewel. The classic country house in the classic country setting.

So this is what I'm turning down. Hannah rested her hands on the steering wheel, her eyes taking in the flow of the land, the way the house was set so perfectly on the low rise above the lake. And above it all, a deep blue sky, broken only by faint wisps of cloud.

Was she crazy?

The Westervelds wouldn't want her intruding into their memory of Sam. She and her mother were an anomaly in Sam's life.

She should go.

Not yet, she thought, putting the car in gear and turning off the key. She wanted to have another look at Sam's place and imagine him here. She wanted to fill in the blank spot of the "before us and after us," the part of Sam's life that had called him back.

As Hannah stepped out of her car she heard the sound of a door slamming shut. She turned in time to see Ethan charge out of the house, buttoning his shirt as he ran.

He slowed down as he saw her, then walked her way, tucking the faded plaid shirt into old, worn jeans.

"Hey, there," he said as he came nearer. "Come to check the place out after all?"

"I was just going for a drive."

He stopped on the other side of her car and leaned on the roof. "You want a tour?"

"No. It looks like you're busy. I was just…" She lifted her chin. "Just curious."

Ethan nodded, drumming his fingers on the roof.

Hannah looked past him to the house with the lake shining in the background. "It's a beautiful spot," she said quietly.

Ethan glanced back in the same direction she'd been looking. "That it is," he agreed. "I spent a lot of hours on that lake. I think I know every drop of water it holds."

"Does the lake have fish?"

"Uncle Sam and I have been trying for the past

couple of years to stock it with trout. My cousins and I used to fish on it."

"Cousins." She digested that thought a moment. "How many are there of you?"

"I was blessed with two parents, Morris and Dot, one sister, Francine, a bunch of girl cousins and two male cousins. Sam, of course, had no kids."

And there it came again. The faint backward slap of dismissal. She and her mother were never a legal part of the Westerveld clan, hence they didn't count.

Did the whole family see her and her mother this way? Some shadowy interlude? A mistake rectified only when Sam returned to the Westerveld bosom and all that messy business back East was cleared out of his life so he could move on?

Did they even think about her and her mother and what had happened to them when Sam left?

Hannah looked back at the house again and an old yearning trembled awake. She remembered Sam talking about the farm. About the garden he used to grow.

One spring, when she was eight, they bought some potting soil, a huge planter and some bedding plants. They planted and watered them. June and July their balcony was a cornucopia of flowers and scents. But best of all, in August, they plucked sun-warmed tomatoes for their salad. Sam made BLTs every night for a week. Hannah easily remembered the sweet tang of those tomatoes.

And she remembered the wistful look on Sam's face when they pulled the dead plant up and took the pot to the Dumpster in the parking lot of the apartment.

This was what he'd been missing. Hannah surveyed the yard, the house, and that perfect little lake behind. Was this why he had stayed away from her and her mother?

To her surprise and dismay, tears pricked her eyes. She turned away, pretending to look at another part of the yard while she swiped the tears from her cheek.

"Did Sam have a garden here?" she asked, trying to sound normal and contained.

"Yeah. Behind the house. But the past couple of years, he didn't do much gardening. Do you want to see it?"

"Look, you have work to do and I'd better get back to town. Thanks for the offer though." She gave him a quick smile and ducked into the car.

But before she put the car in Reverse, she looked at the house again, trying to imagine Sam sitting on the porch, looking out over the lake.

Well, this was it. Her last look at the place he'd come to. She'd probably never see it again.

Hannah sat bolt upright in the bed, pulling herself out of a busy, fretful dream. She blinked as she looked around, her mind trying to make sense of where she was. The light coming into the room was all wrong.

Cheap prints on the wall, thin curtains at the window.

Hannah rubbed her eyes. The motel in Riverbend.

She glanced the clock radio beside her bed and blinked at the numbers.

Eight forty-five in the morning.

She pulled her hands over her face as sleep still dragged at her mind. She couldn't believe she had slept that long. Of course in Toronto the screeching of the GO train past her window in the morning got her up well before her alarm clock rang.

The day slowly registered. The day she was supposed to tell Dan Westerveld that she wouldn't be staying. Yesterday she had done what Lizzie suggested and driven around town. She walked down Main Street, had coffee at the coffee shop, listening to the chitchat of the local people as they wandered in and out. The owner, an attractive woman of indeterminate age, had glanced at her with curiosity from time to time, but had left her alone.

She had driven around some more, but had avoided going down the road with the Farm for Sale sign. A puzzling restlessness had clawed at her, keeping her on the move.

Now it was Sunday morning and this afternoon her plane was leaving. She stretched across the bed, snagged her cell phone off the bed and punched in Lizzie's number again.

Yawning, she walked to the window of the hotel room and tugged one curtain aside. As with all motels, her window looked out over a parking lot, but beyond that she could see a field and above it all the blue bowl of the sky wisped with clouds.

Another beautiful day in Alberta.

She frowned as the phone kept ringing. Where was Lizzie? She had tried to phone Lizzie a couple of times yesterday, but had been shunted to Lizzie's answering system each time. Hannah snapped the phone shut, folding her hand around it as she leaned in the window, her eyes following the path of a hawk in the sky above.

The sprightly tune of Gloria Gaynor's "I Will Survive" jangled from her fist and she snapped open the phone, glancing at the name.

"Taylor. Hello."

"Hey, congratulations, beautiful." Taylor's fake heartiness annoyed her, as it always did. "I heard you inherited half a farm. Lizzie told me not to call you, but I couldn't resist. I'm trying to imagine you slopping hogs and feeding chickens."

His faintly mocking voice irked her, as well. Ever since she had turned Taylor down for a date, he'd treated her with a veiled measure of disdain. Just enough to grate but not enough to call him out on it. "I only get the farm if I stick around for six months, which I'm not."

"You're not? Lizzie said you were moving out there."

Hannah frowned as she tried to make sense of what Taylor was telling her. "Lizzie told you wrong."

"But…I thought… That's why I signed the deal with her and Pete."

"What deal?"

"The salon deal. Lizzie said Pete came in as a partner when she found out you were staying out West. He had a bunch of money he wanted to invest. I signed everything up with her yesterday. She's the new owner."

She couldn't marshal her thoughts as protests, shock, dismay and anger, then fury, fought with each other to be articulated.

"You sold the salon to Lizzie?"

"She and Pete will take possession in a week and move in upstairs. She told me she wanted to tell you herself but I thought I'd call anyway. I was curious about the farming thing. Whatever made you want to stay in redneck land?"

His words simply slipped past her—noises requiring words she couldn't formulate. Shock still held her in its thrall.

Lizzie had done the deal behind her back? Lizzie and Pete now owned the salon? Lizzie and

Pete were going to move into the apartment she had envisioned as her own?

Then, as the enormity of what her friend had done finally registered, she realized she didn't need to talk to Taylor anymore. He had nothing to give her now.

Hannah hesitated in the foyer of the church, her hands clenched at her sides. On the way here, fury at Lizzie's betrayal had taken over the initial shock, keeping her feet and hands ice-cold.

Each time her mind replayed Taylor's conversation, her anger smoldered and grew, seeking an outlet. And she had found it as Lizzie's betrayal resurrected older, deeper betrayals. Alex. Sam.

At least Sam had acknowledged his mistake and had tried to make amends. And as the heat of her anger cooled, it was replaced by a steely determination to take care of herself and not be concerned by what others thought.

Meeting Dan Westerveld at church had not been the plan, but when she had called the Westerveld home and gotten no answer she could only surmise they were here.

But as she entered the foyer, her moment of rebellion lost its punch. What was she doing in a church? She had no right to be here.

Well, she'd just have to go out and wait in the—

"Welcome to our services."

Hannah bit back a startled scream and spun around to face a very friendly, smiling man.

"If you'll wait a moment, I'll find you a place," he said.

Hannah took a step back, waving her hand over her shoulder as if to indicate that someone was waiting for her. "No. That's fine."

"Follow me." The usher checked back to see if she was coming. What else could she do but follow in the wake of his helpfulness into the sanctuary?

A sense of twisted, divine humor assailed her as the usher finally stopped, indicating an empty spot right beside Ethan Westerveld.

Ethan was talking to a young woman beside him. A different one than the girl she'd seen with him in town. As Hannah plunked down beside him, he turned to look at her, but his welcoming expression froze and turned into a polite nod.

The minister greeted the congregation, urging them to rise and sing.

As the music started up, Hannah looked for the proper book. She felt an elbow nudge her and glanced sidelong to see Ethan holding out a book. "Here."

Hannah took the book and, as she opened it, the young woman beside Ethan leaned forward, giving Hannah a once-over and a frown.

Okay, so her jeans and suede jacket over a T-shirt wasn't the best outfit for church, but she hadn't counted on being in the middle of the action. She wasn't going to let this woman intimidate her. Hannah gave her a beatific smile then turned back to her songbook.

The woman pulled back and, though Ethan wasn't looking at her, she caught a flash of a dimple on his cheek. So he thought this was funny?

Maybe another time it might be. But she wasn't about to make a fool of herself in the community in which she was going to be spending the next six months.

Panic gripped her at the thought. Six months. One hundred and eighty-some days. And what about her apartment? Her stuff? Her clothes?

What if Dan said she had waited too long? Had she lost her chance?

Hannah gripped the book as her eyes scanned the music of the song, trying to focus her scattered thoughts.

"…the ripe fruits in the garden," Hannah sang, and her mind immediately sprang to Sam and the farm and his garden.

Her garden now.

She repeated the words, cementing them in her mind. She knew she faced the objections of Ethan and the Westerveld family. With a shake of her head she dismissed the thought. Sam had willed her half of the farm. She would stay—had to stay, thanks to her two-faced friend.

"…the Lord God made them all." She ignored Ethan's sidelong glance as she finished the song and closed the book with a decisive snap.

The congregation settled back down as the minister began to speak about God and how He revealed Himself in nature.

The comment gave her pause as she thought about the changing seasons. How spring was slowly making itself known. She wondered what the farm would look like in a couple of weeks.

"…but what is most amazing, what truly calls us to stop and think is that the God who created this world and this vast universe in all its intricacies, wants to be in a relationship with us." The minister's voice rose, snagging Hannah's wandering attention. "He wants to be a faithful father to us. To love us. That's why He gave His only son. As a sacrifice to pay for our sins."

His words, spoken with such stirring conviction, created a tingle in Hannah's chest. Sam had once told her the story of how God was also the Jesus that came at Christmas and the shepherd from Psalm 23. This had gotten too confusing for Hannah and then her mother told Sam to stop putting fairy tales in Hannah's head.

And slowly Hannah relegated the stories of Jesus and God to the realm of Sleeping Beauty, Cinderella and Bambi. Nice stories, but just that. Stories.

And now this man, in all seriousness, talked

about this same God, the creator of the world, as if He was a father?

Hannah never knew her biological father. Sam was the only father figure in her life. And he had left.

She tried not to fidget as the service went on and when they finally stood for what looked to be the last song, Hannah started looking around the congregation for Dan. She wanted to get this part of the deal over and done with.

"You looking for someone in particular?" Ethan's deep voice pulled her attention to him.

She met his eyes and caught it again, the faintest glimmer of interest. And she felt it again. An answering glint of awareness.

Which was *not* what should be on her mind right now. Being attracted to a man, whom she might be forced to spend six months working with, was not an option.

And then she saw Dan coming down the aisle toward her and she put aside thoughts of Ethan. Hannah waited until Dan came alongside, then screwed up her courage and joined him in the aisle.

"Hannah. Good to see you here." His enthusiasm made her feel like a fraud.

"I've made a decision."

Dan looked over at his wife, Tilly, who seemed vitally interested in what they were saying. "Do you want to go somewhere private?"

"Not really." People would find out soon

enough what her decision was. She gave him a tight smile, hoping he wouldn't catch the hint of desperation in her voice. "I've decided to stay."

mining it. The quieter version of the symphony now
right, she thought, as within reach the buzz of
desperation in her voice. Yeah, she could do very

Chapter Four

❧

"There's a set of clean sheets in the cupboard. Some towels there, as well. You can put your groceries in the fridge." Ethan waited as Hannah glanced around the kitchen, two bags of groceries hanging from her hands. He struggled to keep his voice even, his tone neutral.

He was still processing the implications of Sam's last decision, let alone having this woman staying on the farm. Last night he moved what stuff he could to the holiday trailer his dad kept parked on the yard for storage. He didn't have much to pack up. As for the condition of the house...

Well, he hadn't counted on a woman staying here. She would just have to take it as it is, he thought, forcing himself to ignore the stack of dirty dishes in the sink and the crumbs on the counter from his breakfast this morning.

"I feel bad that I'm kicking you out of your house," Hannah said, setting the bags on the counter. "I can stay in the holiday trailer."

"This is easier." Besides, the condition of the trailer was even sketchier. No one had cleaned the trailer since his nieces and nephews stayed in it last summer.

"Okay." Hannah looked around again. "This is a nice place."

"It needs some cleaning." Ethan scratched his head, wishing he could as easily dispel the low-level headache pressing behind his eyes. "So you going to be okay? Got enough food?" he felt compelled to ask. After all, she was a city girl unaccustomed to living in the country.

"I've got enough for a couple weeks, I think." Her tight smile belied her breezy confidence. "Thanks for showing me around."

"Next time I go to town, I'll let you know. Now that you don't have a car."

He'd had to pick her up from the dealership where she had rented a vehicle. He wondered why she returned it and how she was going to last without a car way out here. "Uncle Dan recommended I give you a small allowance from the farm. Just to keep you in groceries and whatever else you might need. We can settle up for that in…" He let the sentence trail off.

"In six months," Hannah finished for him.

He wasn't going to think that far or notice how she looked around the place—as if mentally figuring out what she could get for it.

He couldn't think about losing this farm. He'd poured too much time and money into it. This farm had been his refuge; his second home as long as he could remember. Though his parents, Morris and Dot, lived and worked in town, Ethan had come to the farm whenever he could. His first vivid memory was of riding with his grandfather on the tractor, pulling the seed drill. First his grandfather and then his uncle had promised him this farm. His father had told him to get something in writing, but he had trusted Uncle Sam.

He should have been more hard-nosed. More businesslike.

Now he was facing the very real prospect of losing half of what he had spent most of his life working toward, and all because he hadn't treated his own uncle like a business partner.

He put the brakes on his thoughts. She needed to stay there six months. She might not last. Concentrate only on today, he reminded himself. He thought he had learned that lesson by now, but obviously he needed reminding.

For now his focus was putting the crop in and getting the cows calved out. When that was done, he could move on to the next thing that needed his attention.

"So, I'm going to be heading out. I've got a few chores to do."

"What kind of chores?"

"You wouldn't be interested." None of the girls he brought to the farm were; why should a city girl be?

She nodded, her expression growing hard. "You're probably right."

He left, carefully closing the door behind him. The sun was sinking below the horizon and he shivered a moment in the chill evening air.

Scout, his faithful dog, jumped up from his usual place by the back door and fell into step beside him, his tail wagging with the eternal optimism of dogs the world over.

"Hey, there," he said, ruffling his dark fur. "Things are going to be different now. We've got someone else on the yard." Ethan glanced back at the house.

Hannah stood in front of one of the windows. He couldn't see her face, only her silhouette as she looked out.

"She's probably wondering what she got herself into," he murmured to his dog. "City girl, out in the middle of nowhere."

The thought gave him some small measure of comfort. She wouldn't last the six months.

He needed to call his lawyer first thing in the morning and get things going. He had no idea where he stood from a legal viewpoint, but he wasn't going to simply roll over and watch years of hard work get siphoned off by Marla Kristoferson's daughter.

Hannah lay in the bed, her hands folded on her stomach, her eyes focused on the ceiling, her thoughts spinning in her head.

What had she done? Was she crazy? What had made her think she could move from the middle of a city of millions out to the country with no one except one resentful man staying in a trailer nearby?

She angled her head to the side, trying to catch some noise, the tiniest note of familiarity.

But nothing. No cars. No trains. No music from rowdy neighbors. No voices outside the building.

A lot of heavy, quiet nothing in a lot of heavy, quiet darkness.

Don't panic. Don't panic, she reminded herself, rolling over onto her side. How could there not be any extra bit of light?

What if she had to go to the bathroom in the middle of the night? Surely she would bump into something, fall and break her neck on her way to turn on the light, and who would be here to hear her? Who would even notice her? She'd be lying on the floor for weeks before anyone discovered her.

Hannah flopped onto her back again, pushing the fear to the side. She was crazy. Certifiable. She knew Ethan was hoping she wouldn't last the full six months. And maybe he was right. Maybe she was too much of a city girl. Maybe she was over-estimating her ability to last. She didn't have to do this, did she?

But she did. She had no choice. The thought slithered like a snake in her belly. After moving out of her mother's apartment, she had made a vow that she was going to be in charge of her own life, that she wasn't going to have circumstances dictate her choices.

And here she was, pushed into a corner like some reluctant rabbit by a friend who wasn't a friend at all. *Snake* was a better word.

She sighed and punched the pillow, taking out her anger at Lizzie on the pillow. Louse. Rotter. Betrayer. Her anger with Lizzie combined with her latent anger with Alex. Whatever happened to faithfulness? To working on relationships?

A high-pitched howl pierced the night and Hannah shot up, looking fearfully around as another howl joined the first. The second one was much closer. Then a third chimed in, their eerie notes slithering down the scale.

From another part of the yard the dog started barking. Ethan's dog, she assumed. Did it know something she didn't know? Was something crouching in the darkness, waiting, watching, its dark red eyes glowing with anticipation?

Suddenly she wished for the quiet.

She lay back on the bed, counting backward from one hundred, like Sam had taught her to do when she was little and afraid of the dark. And as she counted, lying in the house that Sam had lived in up until just a few short weeks ago, it was as if she could hear him talking to her. Telling her it would be okay.

The memory comforted her. She kept counting, out loud, her monotone voice filling the sudden silence.

Which was broken by the creaking sound of a door opening downstairs.

Her heart pitched into her throat. That something she had thought was waiting, was now trying to get into the house.

But she had locked the door.

What was she supposed to do? Call the police?

Right. And how far away were they? By the time they got here she could be buried in the back forty, the murderer laughing all the way to the border.

Hannah grabbed her housecoat and pulled it on over her pajamas, determined that she was not going to be murdered in her bed. Then she saw a broom leaning against the door.

Pretty flimsy protection, but it was better than going down empty-handed.

And where was that dog? Shouldn't he have been barking up a storm? Or maybe the dog was already dead. Maybe the murderer had gotten to Ethan and the dog first.

Too many horror movies, Hannah reminded herself, trying to corral her runaway thoughts. There's a reasonable explanation for everything. It could be Ethan. Whom she would cheerfully hit with the broom. Had to be Ethan. But why would he be sneaking around?

Then she heard another creak downstairs and all coherent thought fled. Someone was in the house she had locked up securely and double-checked. And she was all alone.

She eased open the door, wincing as it creaked into the silence. She stopped, waited.

But as she listened, her ears hyperaware, she heard the sound of the floor creaking under cautious footsteps.

She might have a chance of getting out of the house. And then what? Run mindlessly through the yard as the intruder ran after her brandishing a knife?

Should she be praying right now?

If You help me through this, Lord, I'll go to church, she promised, drawing in a long slow breath for courage. *I can't promise much more than that.*

She paused, wondering if she would hear an answer. Then, realizing she couldn't leave everything up to God, she slowly worked her way down the stairs, her hands clutching the broom in a death grip. She kept her back to the wall, her eyes darting around the gloom. The only things she could make out were the hulking forms of the couch and chair in the living room.

Oh Lord, I just want to get out of here alive. That's all. Her prayer was instinctive but, at the moment, heartfelt.

The sudden flash of light blinded her. She held up her broom, took a panicked step toward the door and tripped over the hem of her housecoat.

This is it, she thought as she fell, a dark figure hovering over her. This is how it ends. In an isolated country house, in the middle of nowhere.

Hands caught her, hauled her up.

She made an ineffectual jab with her broom at the dark figure holding on to her.

"Hey, easy with that," the intruder said, blocking her jab with one arm. "Someone could get hurt."

Hannah blinked at the sound of the voice.

Ethan.

Chapter Five

"What are you doing?" he asked, still holding on to her.

She pushed at his hands, stumbled again as he let go of her. But as she regained her balance, fear gave way to anger.

"No. You don't get to ask questions. I get to ask questions." She blinked, her eyes adjusting slowly to the beam of light shining down on the entranceway. She dropped the broom and yanked on the ties of her housecoat. "And my question is, what are you doing here?"

"I forgot my coat."

"But I locked the house."

He held up a key chain. "Sorry. I have my own keys."

Hannah's overworked heart still hammered in her chest. "You shouldn't do that. I thought—"

"You thought you were going to beat me to death with that broom."

"That thought did cross my mind," she said, folding her arms over her chest. "You scared me half to death."

"Sorry." Ethan's smile faded away and Hannah felt a moment's regret. She hadn't seen him smile since the first time they had met on the street corner. "Did you really think I was burglar?"

He had adopted a more neutral expression, but she knew he was still laughing at her.

"What else was I supposed to think? Usually when a person locks their door, it stays locked."

"And here I was worried about waking you."

Hannah swallowed, her heart finally returning to a more normal rhythm. "Well, I wasn't sleeping."

"Coyotes keep you awake?"

"Was that what that howling was?"

"Yeah. They were actually pretty quiet tonight. Usually they're singing all around the yard."

Was she imagining it or did his voice hold an extra note of glee?

"I'm sure I'll get used to it." She didn't have a choice now, did she? "So what did you want?"

"My coat." Ethan slipped it over his shirt and shoved his hands in the pockets. "Sorry I disturbed you. I won't do it again."

His casual dismissal, on top of the roller coaster of emotions she had just endured, kindled her anger.

"Maybe you should give me the keys and then it won't happen again," she said.

Ethan stopped, slowly pivoted back to face her, his expression grim. "What did you just ask me?"

"I'm sure you heard me. You're only a couple of feet away."

Ethan closed the small distance and came to stand directly in front of her. If he was trying to intimidate her, he was almost succeeding. Almost.

"This farm isn't yours. Yet. And if I have my way, you won't be able to lay any claim to it. But until the title is transferred to your name, I have as much right to come and go in this house as you do. I'm sorry I scared you and in the future I'll try not to disturb you. I'll respect your privacy, but I'm not giving you the keys to my house."

Hannah tried to stare him down, her anger with him shifting and settling. "Fine. But I'm holding you to the promise to respect my privacy."

"You don't need to. Unlike most women, I keep my promises."

She didn't know where that came from. "Then you are a rarity among men," she snapped back. "A lot of the men I know don't comprehend the meaning of the word."

They faced each other down, their words heavy with unspoken meaning.

"I'll leave the dog here for you. He'll keep the

coyotes at bay." Then Ethan gave a short laugh, turned and left, closing the door quietly behind him.

Hannah leaned against the wall, her arms and legs rubbery with delayed reaction.

"See," she said to Scout, who was standing beside her, filling the ensuing silence with false bravado. "Nothing to be afraid of after all."

Something warm was lying alongside her.

Hannah slowly opened her eyes, feeling disoriented. The room was full of light. The door was all wrong. Where was she?

She heard a light snuffle, then a sigh and her heart jumped again as she sat up, pulling her blankets up and around herself.

A pair of brown eyes, almost buried in long brown hair stared back at her. A pink tongue hung out of its mouth.

Scout. The dog angled its head to one side, as if studying her.

"I'm guessing you're used to sleeping here," she said, reaching out to stroke its head. "But I'm afraid that you're going to have to get unused to this. I don't share my bed with anyone, or anything. Period. You understand?"

The dog turned his head, as if listening for something only he could hear.

"More coyotes out there?" Hannah fondled his ears, smiling.

But the dog jumped off the bed and stood by her bedroom door, whining.

Hannah got up and checked her watch. "Six o'clock? Are you kidding me?" It was too light for six o'clock. It was too *early* for six o'clock.

She trudged to the door, opened it, and the dog scampered out of the room, his feet pounding down the stairs.

"Hey, there, Scout," she heard Ethan whisper.

"You don't need to be all quiet. I'm awake," Hannah called, pushing down her annoyance that he had gained entrée into the house yet again.

"Good morning," Ethan yelled from below. "I've just come to get my dog."

"I thought I locked the door," Hannah yelled back, her anger from the previous night spilling over into her voice.

"Why don't you come down here so we don't have to yell back and forth at each other," Ethan shouted.

"No." Bad enough that he had seen her in her ratty housecoat last night. She wasn't about to repeat the performance. Next time he saw her, she was going to be fully dressed.

"If you want eggs for breakfast, you'll have to wait," Ethan said.

"For what?"

"I have to gather them yet."

"From where?"

"The grocery store."

"What?"

"I'm kidding. I have to get them from the chickens."

Hannah pulled her housecoat closer around her and shook her head. Egg-laying chickens? What was this, the Waltons come to life?

"Do you want some milk?" he asked.

"No. Thanks. Eggs will be fine though." She didn't want to contemplate the milk's origin. She waited until she heard the door close then hurried downstairs and, even though Ethan had the keys, she locked it once more. Maybe he would get the hint.

She pulled aside the thin curtain covering the window of the door and watched as Ethan strode across the yard, his hands in his pockets, his stride sure, his dog trotting alongside him, looking up with what looked suspiciously like adoration.

A man and his dog. A man in charge of his world.

A pain in the neck.

Hannah scurried upstairs and showered. She pulled her still-damp hair back and covered it with a bandanna. Makeup? Nope. She was out in the country and she wasn't going to dress up for some Neanderthal who broke into people's houses and scared them half to death.

She returned to the bedroom and finished unpacking the precious few clothes she had taken along. Hannah had left a message with her landlord to get Lizzie to pack up her stuff and put it in storage. That was the least her supposed friend could do for her. There was no way she was going to call Lizzie herself. Not now. Maybe never.

Thoughts of Lizzie rekindled her anger at her friend's betrayal. She couldn't imagine how her so-called friend could have done that to her.

She pressed her hand to her stomach, stilling the fluttering nerves taking up permanent residence there.

"People have let you down before. You've moved enough times in your life," she reminded herself, talking aloud to fill the heavy silence. "This is nothing new."

Hannah fluffed the down pillows of the bed and pulled the sheet over them, trying to calm herself. As she tugged the quilt straight, she ran her fingers over the old, faded blocks. Some of the stitching was coming loose. She looked more closely at the material and smiled. It had been sewn from odds and ends of material. Some polyester, some cotton. Maybe even old clothes?

Had Sam's mother sewed this?

Hannah smoothed an errant wrinkle, feeling a touch of melancholy at the unspoken history inherent in this quilt and this house. The bed with its heavy wooden headboard looked antique, as did the dresser with its oval mirror framed in wood and the hoop-backed chair beside it.

Hannah walked over to the dresser and ran her finger over the dust, wondering how long since someone had come to clean.

She opened the drawers. The first few were empty, but in the bottom drawer on the right side she found a single sock and a box.

She lifted the box out, stifling the feeling that she was snooping. Inside the box were papers, envelopes and some old bills. She was about to close the box when she saw the corner of a photo peeking out of one of the envelopes. Carefully she pulled out the curling picture and her heart clenched. The picture was an old, faded shot of her holding up a handful of dandelions and grinning at the camera.

Hannah studied the picture, raking through her past, and slowly the memory surfaced.

It was a Saturday morning and Hannah had been wandering listlessly around the apartment, uncertain if she should turn on the television and risk waking her mother, who still slept. She didn't dare leave the apartment, because Sam had left early that morning and had taken the single set of keys with him.

But the sun outside beckoned, with the alluring promise of a clear, sunny day. And she ached to be out there.

So she had given in to the impulse and just as she was leaving the apartment building, Sam had pulled up in his old, battered pickup truck.

He drove her to the park and, on the way, they bought a disposable camera. They had taken turns taking pictures of each other. Some goofy, many out of focus. But this one had turned out perfect, according to Sam. When it came back from the developer, Sam had bought a cheap plastic frame and hung it on the wall.

One evening her mother had a party and the picture had been knocked off the wall. The frame broke and the picture was taken out and Hannah never saw it again.

She touched the picture now, melancholy and old memories washing over her. Life with her mother had not been easy, especially after Sam left. Now her mother was gone. And so was Sam.

Hannah felt as if she stood on the edge of a vast river of sorrow and loss. If she leaned too far forward, she would get sucked in. She couldn't let herself fall; there was no one to pull her out.

She pushed the picture back in the envelope then closed the lid on the box and the onslaught of the past.

Best get to work, she thought, grabbing the box and placing it in the closet of her room. Keep her body busy and her mind would be occupied, as well.

A quick tour of the rest of the house showed her that it hadn't been cleaned for a while, either.

She knelt down and opened the cupboard door. Underneath the sink, she found an old ice-cream pail, some rags and, goodness, a brand-new bottle of all-purpose cleaner.

Before she could fill the pail, however, she had to clean out the sink, still filled with an assortment of dirty dishes. And before she could wash them, she had to clean off the counter to find a place to put the clean dishes.

Bachelors, she thought with disgust as she glanced out the large, dusty and speckled window above the sink. And stopped what she was doing.

The yard of the house was surrounded by poplar trees that held just a hint of green in their leaves. In a few weeks, the yard would be completely secluded, she thought. But for now, through the trees she saw the large red barn she had seen when she first came to the farm and beyond that, open fields that rolled and flowed, broken by ragged lines of spruce and poplar trees.

And not one single house.

The sheer vastness of the space created a sense of vertigo and she grabbed the edge of the counter to steady herself.

Behind her, the only sounds in the house were the faint humming of the refrigerator and the muted tick of a clock. No other noise broke the silence that pressed in on her ears with a force that almost hurt.

She swallowed a bubble of panic. It's okay. Everything is okay, she reminded herself. You're just a little farther away from people, that's all.

The ringing of the phone broke the moment. With a thankful start, she wiped her hands on an old, gray hand towel, and glanced around the kitchen. Where was the phone? She waited, listened, then followed the sound through the dining room, turned left and walked through an arched entrance into the living room. The ringing grew louder, but she still couldn't place its location.

She glanced around the room, taking in the stone fireplace, hardwood floor, wooden rocking chair, battered coffee table and a lone couch parked in front of a plasma television that took up most of the wall.

Another insistent ring and she homed in on the couch. She found the phone on the couch, on top of a stack of magazines, which lay on top of an old, faded afghan.

She punched the on button and said hello as she flipped the towel over her shoulder and gathered up the magazines with her free hand. The living room looked as if it had been lived in.

"Who is this?" a female voice demanded.

"Actually, that's my line," Hannah said absently as she took stock of the mess in this room. Whoever this decidedly angry woman was, Hannah was sure she was less than impressed that a woman was staying in Ethan's house.

"Well, this is Alana. Where is Ethan?"

Alana could use some lessons in politeness,

Hannah thought, tucking the phone under her ear as she set the stack of magazines on the coffee table.

"He's outside."

"When he comes in, tell him to call me."

"I'll do that." As soon as the words left Hannah's mouth, she regretted being so snippy. She didn't have to lower herself to this girl's standard, but she couldn't help it. Even though she was, at the moment, cleaning up Ethan's house, she didn't like being treated like hired help. "Does he know your number?"

"He should. And who are you, anyway?" Alana's curiosity had finally got the upper hand.

"Shirttail relative," Hannah replied as she bent over to pull a plate from under the coffee table. She turned up her nose at the tomato sauce crusting the edges and at the dust and mess. Bachelors.

"Whatever. Like I said, tell him I called." And Alana hung up.

Hannah pulled a face at the phone and brought it and the dirty plate back to the kitchen. The phone ended up on the kitchen table, the plate in the sink.

As Hannah washed, her eyes drifted to the view out of the kitchen window.

Still there. Still empty.

No, wait. A tall figure came out of the barn, a large dog beside him. Ethan, she thought with a flush of relief. He cradled his hat in his hands as he walked toward the house.

She ducked her head, concentrating on cleaning the dishes. She laid another towel out on the counter and put the clean dishes there to dry.

A few moments later she heard the creak of the door and a dull thud as it slammed shut. Footsteps and then Ethan was in the kitchen.

"I brought you some eggs," he said. "They need to get washed though." He walked over to the sink, his presence dominating the small space. He wore a pale brown shirt today, the sleeves rolled up over his forearms, and blue jeans. His blond hair was tamed down but Hannah saw a ridge in his hair from his hat. A light frown of concentration creased his forehead as he pulled a plastic bowl out of the cupboard.

Hannah resisted the urge to pull herself back as he reached over and ran water over the eggs. He stood too close, which made her uncomfortable, and when he turned his head to look at her and his gaze met hers, she felt a shiver of awareness.

She caught herself in time, forcing her attention down to the bowl.

Six brown eggs, two white and two pale blue eggs lay inside, and curiosity took the upper hand. "What kind of bird lays those eggs?"

In all the years she had been shopping, she had never seen blue chicken eggs.

"A chicken."

Hannah bristled at his patronizing tone and the

lazy grin she could see in her peripheral vision. "I got that part. I guess I was wondering about the blue eggs. Also chicken?"

"Banty."

She frowned.

"A type of chicken," Ethan explained, reaching past her to grab one of the scrub brushes lying on the counter. "They kind of do their own thing. Lay eggs wherever they want. I found these tucked in a corner of a granary."

"They're edible?"

"Probably more edible than what you buy in a store," he said as he scrubbed the eggs.

His tone held an edge of something she couldn't quite define, nor wanted to analyze. She knew he resented her presence but, though staying here was hardly her first choice, the reality was right now she had no choice.

But she wished he wouldn't stand so close—he made her uncomfortable. Still, she wasn't going to move away and let him know that. Ethan seemed the kind of person that you faced head-on, not backed away from.

"By the way, I got a phone call from a friend of yours. Someone named Alana." She shot him a sidelong glance but his expression didn't change. "She sounded like she really wanted you to call her back."

Ethan shrugged and laid the eggs on a plate to dry.

"She said you would know her number," Hannah continued.

"Okay."

"While we're on the topic, do you want me to field your phone calls?"

"Is it too much trouble?" Ethan's tone held that faint edge of mockery and the fine hairs on the back of her neck rose again. "I don't have a phone in the trailer."

"No, no trouble at all," she said, forcing her attention back to the dishes she was washing. "Are you done?"

"Yeah, I am." He shook the excess moisture from his hands, the water drops joining the myriad of spots on the window above the sink. "Enjoy the eggs." He wiped his hands on his pants and left.

Hannah clenched the dish brush tighter, wondering how she was supposed to get through six months living next door to this man.

I have no other choice.

Lizzie's defection had made that abundantly clear.

She supposed she should be thankful she at least had a place to stay for now. But as she chanced another look out the speckled window, the fear she had felt last night prowling around the periphery of her mind slithered back. Six months. Stuck out here so far away from civilization. Did she really think she could last?

You have no choice. Lizzie took that choice away from you.

Hannah closed her mind to that insistent voice and the frustrated anger it resurrected. She had spent enough years trailing along behind her mother as Marla moved from place to place, from man to man. Until she moved out on her own, Hannah had had no choice in how they lived and where.

Foolishly, she had thought partnering up with Lizzie would give her some measure of independence and choice, but that was taken out of her hands, as well.

If she believed in the Westerveld God, she would be asking Him what was going on. Instead, she was going to make the best of her current situation and turn it to her advantage.

Hannah finished drying the dishes and, after poking through a few of the cupboards haphazardly filled with groceries and dishes, she found a place for them.

She sighed. It was as if each small chore she did created a bigger chore. The entire house needed a good cleaning and rearranging.

Accept the things you can't change, change the things you can, she reminded herself. These words were what had got her through changes in school, changes in friends, in location and situation. They got her through those weeks post-Alex when she wondered if any guy was worth turning into a fool over. They would get her through Lizzie's duplicity, as well.

Some more exploring led her to a vacuum cleaner and, surprise, surprise, the bag wasn't overflowing. In fact, it was still new.

Three hours later she had the downstairs cleaned and vacuumed, the furniture dusted and the insides of the windows washed. The growling of her stomach was a vivid reminder that she hadn't eaten breakfast yet this morning.

The eggs still sat on the plate on the counter. She could make an omelet, but a quick review of the refrigerator showed her how limited her options were. Guess it was scrambled eggs and a piece of bread from the half a loaf she found tucked away in the breadbox on the counter.

Her search through the disorganized cupboards for a frying pan only served to raise another work project.

Fifteen minutes later, her eggs were finished and her stomach no longer growled.

And she was tired of housecleaning.

She looked outside. The sun shone and a light breeze tossed the branches of the trees around. She slipped on her sandals and headed out the door.

Then stopped.

The cracked sidewalk was only twenty feet long and after that—dust and dirt.

The breeze tossed her hair around so she pulled

it back and anchored it with a ponytail tie she dug from her pocket. As she looked around, a shiver of anxiety crawled up her neck at the space spread out before her.

And, as she had noted in the house, the immense quiet. Other than the warbling, lilting melody of one bird and the sibilant hiss of the breeze through the trees, no other sound of civilization filled the air.

No trucks, no cars.

She dropped her head back and saw, far, far above her, the white contrail of a jet engine scratching the hard, blue sky. She remembered looking down from the plane when she flew here, absently taking note of the open space below her.

Never, in any of her wildest dreams, had she imagined herself standing down here, stranded in this vast emptiness.

Emptiness. The word rolled around in her brain, echoing.

Don't panic. Don't panic. Lots of people live out here and do just fine. This is only for six months. Get moving, get doing something. Don't stand here and let life overwhelm you.

She took a breath, then a step, another breath, another step and soon she was at the end of the sidewalk and walking over the ground. She didn't have a destination in mind. For now, she was moving, taking charge. Exploring this new place life had dropped her in. How often had she done the same when she and her mother moved to a new neighborhood? While her mother slept or worked, Hannah would find her bearings by first surveying the new apartment building, then the neighborhood, determining the boundaries of where she felt safe and comfortable.

Out of the corner of her eye she saw a movement. Something large and brown. Her heart jumped but as she turned, she realized it was her sleeping companion.

Scout. Ethan's dog.

He bounded toward her, his tongue hanging out, looking as if he was truly happy to see her.

"Hey, there," Hannah said, bending down to ruffle the fur at his neck. "Do you want to keep me company while I walk?" she asked the dog, scratching behind both his ears at once.

"Be careful, he's the world's worst mooch."

Ethan's voice made her jump, which made her annoyed that she was so skittish. She blamed it on the unfamiliarity of her surroundings and the events of the past few days.

"Pay too much attention to him and you won't be able to get rid of him," Ethan continued.

Hannah fondled Scout's ears, smiling at the dog. "I don't mind if he tags along."

"Where are you going?" Ethan was right beside her now. He was holding something in a rag, wiping it as he talked.

Hannah got to her feet, shading her hand against the sun as she looked up at Ethan.

"Just exploring. Hope that's okay."

"*Mi casa es su casa*, and that's pretty literal."

She got it.

"Now I hope you don't mind if I go and use the phone in the house. I need to call the dealership about this part." He held up something metal and shiny.

Hannah waved her hand as if granting him permission. "You don't need to ask me. It's your house."

"Sort of."

"Right. *Mi casa es su casa*." This was going to take some getting used to. Technically she didn't own anything yet; in six months, half of this could be hers. Boggled the mind actually.

"By the way, if you're going to go exploring, you should know that some of the cows have calved already," Ethan was saying. "Keep your eye on one. Number fifty-five. She can be real miserable the first couple weeks after she calves. You might want to steer clear of her. She'll put the run on you if you get too close to her calf."

"Thanks for the tip." As if she was going to saunter around a cow pasture. "Anyplace off-limits?"

He gave her an odd look. "No. Except I would appreciate it if you didn't start tidying up my trailer."

She held up her hand. "Trust me. The house is challenge enough."

Ethan nodded his head, then left. He was halfway to the house when he glanced over his shoulder and whistled for the dog.

But Scout stayed beside Hannah.

"You'd better go with your boss," Hannah said, nudging him toward Ethan.

Scout looked toward Ethan, then at Hannah, a whine whistling in his throat.

"Scout. C'mon."

The dog took a few steps toward Ethan, then came back to Hannah, licked her hand as if in apology, whined a bit more then trotted off toward his master.

"What's the matter with you?" she heard Ethan scolding his dog.

Hannah felt oddly comforted by Scout's indecision. She'd never had a dog of her own. Looked like she might be sharing this one.

Chapter Six

Ethan glanced out the kitchen window. From his vantage point he could see Hannah heading toward the road. Looked like he had a few minutes. If he watched while he talked, he'd be okay.

He found the number in the phone book and dialed it, returning to the window to keep watch.

"Hello. I'd like to speak to Jace Scholte." He drummed his fingers on the counter while he waited. Hannah disappeared around the bend of the driveway. A city girl like her wouldn't stray too far off the beaten path so he might not have much time.

"Hello, Ethan," boomed a jovial voice into the telephone. "How are you coping?"

"You know, just get through each day."

"Got your crop in?" Jace asked.

Ethan chatted inanely with Jace, touching on the usual farmer talk that created a distance from emotions. The weather, commodity prices, seeding time, calving. While he chatted, Scout wandered into the kitchen and dropped onto his favorite spot, the rug in front of the kitchen sink. Ethan wondered what Hannah would think of that. He hadn't seen the counters so clean and the sink so shiny since his mom and cousin Janie had come the weekend Sam had been expected home from the hospital. They had cleaned and polished and tut-tutted about the mess the entire time they were scurrying around the house. Ethan glanced out the window again. No Hannah. "Actually, Jace, the reason I'm calling you is this will of Sam's. I need to contest it."

Jace's sigh spoke volumes.

"You know as well as I do that Sam changed that will," Ethan pressed. "I don't know what caused him to do that or why, but in every copy of every will he ever made he willed the farm to me."

"You know this is going to cost money and I can't guarantee success. We're either going to have to show undue influence in the writing of the will or question Sam's competence at the time of the change. The family isn't going to appreciate that...."

"I don't think the family appreciates him giving a complete stranger half of his farm right now, anyway. Look, I don't want to appear ungrateful and greedy," Ethan said, trying to explain his actions, "but you know how much work and money I put into this place. I spent a lot of winters as a rig worker, putting in lousy shifts and lousy hours just to keep this farm afloat…." He stopped there as the memories threatened to cloud his current reality.

The entire time he'd been pouring money into this farm, he had never expected anything in return, other than to be able to someday run a solvent farm with his uncle Sam. He and Sam had never written anything up to that effect. They were family. What could have gone wrong?

Everything, it seemed.

Ethan pushed back the low-level panic hovering on the edges of his mind since the reading of the will. He didn't want frustration with Sam to overshadow his genuine grief, but seeing Hannah in this house, walking around this farm, brought up a mixture of disloyal emotions that he prayed every day would go away. Unfortunately, they didn't.

"Are you sure you want to do this, Ethan? It could turn out messy."

Ethan's mind jumped six months ahead. He could already picture the farm sale, see the assets laid out for everyone to pick over.

Because he knew, after all the work he had done to get the farm where it was now, there was no way he could afford to buy half of this farm—not at current land prices. But he also knew of any number of well-established farmers who would jump at the opportunity to buy even half.

"I need you to go ahead with this, Jace."

While he spoke he saw his dog lift his head and give him a mournful look. It was as if Scout was warning him. Ethan turned his back on the dog.

"You can't make a deal with this girl?" Jace asked. "I understand she has to stick around six months to get half of the farm."

"I could try offering her some money. There's room left on my operating loan. Would end up being cheaper in the long run than trying to buy back half of the farm."

"Or you could marry her—then you'd both own the whole farm."

"That's not even remotely humorous," Ethan snapped. As if he would go down that road again anytime soon.

"Sorry. Just trying to lay out all your legal options."

"Let's go with my first choice, okay?"

"If that's what you want to do. I'll get the necessary documents in order," Jace said. "You'll have to come in and sign them and we'll take it from there."

"Thanks, Jace. We'll stay in touch." As Ethan hung up the phone he looked out the window again. Still no Hannah, thank goodness.

He dialed the tractor dealership and minutes later was enmeshed in problems of a more immediate nature. He had to get his big tractor going in the next couple of days if he wanted to get his crop in on time. The smaller tractor he used to feed cows couldn't pull the larger implements. Thankfully, the conditions were still perfect and there was no rain in the forecast.

At least some things were going his way.

He was glad he had taken care of the previous phone call while Hannah was out of the house. He thought of what Jace had told him and wondered if he stood even the smallest sliver of a chance.

Declaring undue influence wouldn't work, because neither Hannah nor her mother were near Sam while he wrote up the will, and Ethan would certainly not have recommended Sam's unusual action.

As for incompetence?

Ethan shoved his hand through his hair trying banish thoughts of the family's reaction to what would be perceived as disloyalty to Sam and Sam's memory.

But other than contesting the will, what other options were available to him?

Jace's first suggestion slipped into his mind. Maybe he could offer her some money. He knew she was less than thrilled to be staying here. Surely she would jump at the chance to get a few thousand dollars up front rather than have to stay here?

After all, it had worked with her mother. Why not with her?

Hannah stood on the porch and wrapped her arms around herself as she watched the sun rise up from the horizon. Another day and another night. Only one hundred and eighty left to go.

The other creatures up this early were birds and chickens, of course. She heard them crowing faintly in the distance.

Five-thirty was way too early to be up and about, but she was still on Eastern time. Back in Toronto, it was seven-thirty and she would have been on the subway, heading toward work and Lizzie.

At the thought of her old friend, a storm of anger and betrayal gathered in Hannah's head, pressing against her temples. How could Lizzie have done this to her? How could she have turned on her so easily and quickly? As if the friendship of the past few years and all the work Hannah had done counted for nothing?

She tried to corral the swirling thoughts, control them and calm them. She had to let go, look ahead to the future and whatever that might bring. As a young girl she had spent many an hour hoping, praying Sam would come back so their life could go back to normal and it hadn't. Looking back served no purpose.

So she could maybe do some exploring of the place Sam's guilt had left her. She had spent all of the day and most of the evening cleaning and washing everything she could in the house. The work had made the house more familiar to her and when she had trudged upstairs and crawled between the freshly washed sheets, she felt a tiny sense of ownership, an entirely new feeling for her.

She passed Ethan's trailer, pleased to note that the curtains were still drawn. Obviously still sleeping, she thought, mentally patting herself on the back.

She came to the driveway and a few minutes later Hannah boldly strode where she hadn't before—up the road toward the hill she had only glanced at yesterday. This time, Scout was with her, which gave her some small comfort. She listened to the quiet, trying to identify sounds—any sound. The only noise was the chirping of birds, but as she listened she was able to separate the melodies. One had a light, cheerful note. Then, as she listened she heard another song, this one lower, like someone blowing across a pop bottle. Once, twice, pause then another longer note.

Hannah felt a touch of melancholy at the mournful sound. When she first heard the bird in Toronto, Sam had told her they were mourning doves. Which seemed appropriate now. She wondered what the other birds were. Maybe she could take up birding. That could occupy about sixty minutes of each day, leaving her approximately nine hundred and some to go.

She got to the top of the hill, stopped and turned around.

From this vantage point she could look back over the farm. She surveyed the land, taking in the small lake behind the house, edged by brown fields and delineated by rows of trees. The country lay like a patchwork below her. Looking the other way, she caught a glimpse of another house and some large buildings beside it. At least there were other people living here, though the thought made Hannah laugh.

Neighbors who lived two miles away instead of ten feet.

She hugged herself against an onslaught of goose bumps. The space and the emptiness of the landscape made her feel disoriented, the way she used to feel when she'd gone one too many rounds on the merry-go-round at the playground. Her entire life had shifted and rearranged and she wasn't sure where her footing was.

Do you really think you can stay out here?

And what other choice did she have?

You've been over this road too many times. You have to make the best of it.

And once again her anger with Lizzie pushed to the forefront. Lizzie, who had forced her into the situation. From there her anger shifted to Sam, who had only realized what he had done to her too late.

She took a slow breath. She had to stop living in the past.

Hannah turned and headed back to the farm. It was mid-April now. Six months would bring her to mid-October. Had Sam assumed that the clock would start ticking the day Hannah made her decision?

She made a mental note to talk to Dan about the timeline.

So, what could she do to keep herself busy during these six months? Would it violate the terms of the will if she got a job?

And how are you supposed to get to town, ninny?

Town was a twenty-minute drive away. She had no vehicle because she didn't want to waste money renting a car for six months.

Ethan had said he'd give her an allowance, but she had to find a way to make herself useful.

Ethan grabbed the milk pail filled with warm water, stepped out of the trailer and looked across the yard to the row of trees dividing the farmhouse from the rest of the yard, regretting his impulse to let Scout stay with Hannah again.

He assumed she might feel safer with the dog,

so last night he had asked her if Scout could stay with her. Her speedy yes had proved his assumption correct.

But that meant that he was now without the company of his dog.

Just in case Hannah had put the dog out this morning, he gave a sharp whistle and waited a moment, but no goofy animal came bounding across the yard toward him.

By the time he got to the barn, Angel, the faithful milk cow, was waiting for him, her head hanging over the gate separating the barn from the corrals. Her soft brown eyes fringed with long eyelashes looked at him expectantly.

"Hey, girl," he said, "how are you this morning?" He carefully hung the milk pail on the hook, scooped some grain into her feeding trough and opened the gate.

Angel trotted into the barn and stuck her head into the stanchion. She knew her part in this little choreography. For the past five years, Ethan had milked her and before that, Uncle Sam and Ethan had taken turns milking Angel and Angel's mother.

As part of his early-morning routine, Ethan turned on the dusty radio resting on a shelf beside the stanchion, pulled his stool up to Angel's side and started milking. For as long as Ethan could remember, Grandpa Westerveld had listened to the early-morning market reports while milking the family cow. The steady drone of the announcer listing off the prices for feed wheat, oats, fat calves and feeder hogs was as much a part of Ethan's memories as his grandfather, face buried in the flank of a beige-brown Jersey cow, his hands barely moving as he filled the pail.

Angel, the current milk cow, was a direct descendant of that milk cow and had just had her third calf, also a female, purebred Jersey. This calf looked like a likely replacement for Angel, who was getting on in years herself.

"Hey, girl, you think your baby will train up as easily as you did?" he said, talking quietly to her as he often did. Angel had been the sounding board for Ethan's struggles when Sam was ill, when Colby had humiliated him so publicly. Angel had listened to his plans for the sixty acres in the back of the home quarter, what he was going to seed on the land adjoining the farm, the two quarters across the road and the two quarters he and Sam had jointly purchased only five years previous.

"Now there's a whole different set of troubles I can dump on you," Ethan murmured, his hands easily taking up the rhythm he had learned from his grandfather. "Trouble is, I don't have a clue how to get myself untangled from all of this. I'm well and truly stuck and all because I trusted Sam too much." Ethan sighed, wishing that his thoughts didn't persistently return to Hannah and the farm and Sam. He had lain awake half of the night feeling like a gerbil on an exercise wheel.

If he challenged the will he ran the risk of making the family angry. If he didn't, he stood to lose everything he had worked so hard for. And he couldn't roll over and let his hard work get auctioned off in six months.

And around and around he went.

"I should have taken the time to draw up that partnership agreement Dad and Jace had been nagging at me to get done. But no, I was too busy getting the crop in, putting up hay, harvesting, working in the oil fields in the winter to make some extra money and then, come spring, start all over again. And what did my trust get me? It got me Miss Hannah Kristoferson. Answering my phone and cleaning my house. And why does she think she's doing me any favors doing that? Of course, she's not doing this for anyone but herself. That's why she ended up on the farm in the first place. How did she put it? I have to take care of myself. Well, she's doing a real good job of that. My new partner. Fat lot of good she's going to do me. Drain on the bank account. That's what she's going to be."

He glared down at the foamy milk in the pail and forced himself to relax. Delivering a tirade to an uncomplaining and uncritical cow could be considered therapy…or the actions of a crazy man.

But what else could he do? Complain to Uncle Dan? He'd had nothing to do with Uncle Sam changing his will. His dad, ever the practical Westerveld, would simply tell Ethan that he should have drawn up a partnership agreement.

The aunts would only commiserate and tell him to trust in God.

Which elicited another sigh.

Of late, trusting in God was not his strong point. When he was younger, he read his Bible regularly, prayed often. But working on the rigs had drawn him out of a more devoted lifestyle and dating Colby hadn't helped. Though she had been raised in the church as he was, she attended only sporadically.

After she dumped him, Ethan had lain low, preferring to lick his wounds in private. Only in the past half year, with encouragement from Sam, had he started attending church. Sam told Ethan to learn from Sam's own mistakes. He had told Ethan about how he had stayed away from God while he was living out East in Toronto, with Hannah's mother, and it didn't work. That God had called him back home and back to Himself.

And, when Sam was in the hospital, he would ask Ethan to read to him from the Bible. Sam's death had rocked Ethan's world in more ways than one, but talking to the minister helped him deal with the emotional repercussions.

As for the financial...

And he was back at the beginning.

An old mother cat and her four small kittens drifted into view and settled in a slant of light coming into the barn, a few feet away from Ethan and Angel.

"Good morning," Ethan said quietly, turning his head to look at the group, thankful for the diversion. "You guys come to mooch some milk off me?" He kept milking, watching the cats as the market news provided a backdrop to the sound of the milk squirting into the pail.

The only response he got from the mother cat was a yawn. The kittens tumbled over one another, batting their paws and wrestling.

Ethan directed a stream of milk toward the mother cat. She shook her head, then opened her mouth, drinking as fast as she could.

One kitten stopped its play, then sidled over to its mother.

Ethan sent another squirt of milk their way and laughed as the kitten tried to get some, as well.

"Don't be such a mooch," he said.

Ethan directed another squirt of milk at the cat as he scolded the little kitten. "You're taking more than you deserve, you little freeloader. On this farm you gotta pull your weight, right? You got to earn your keep. We got enough freeloaders on this farm right now. Maybe I should call you Hannah. Or Marla, after her mother."

The kitten ignored him and batted at the milk. But this time it figured out what to do and started drinking like its mother.

The other kittens stopped their play, watching their littermate. One trotted over and pushed it down. Ethan sprayed it, too. It jumped sideways; its back arched, but then it started licking the milk on its fur. This one was a faster learner and soon was sitting on its haunches trying to drink, as well. Ethan didn't mind sharing with the kittens. He already had more milk than he could drink. Maybe Hannah would want some.

The thought of Hannah elicited another sigh.

Maybe calling her a freeloader was a bit strong, but how else could he look at the situation? She had done nothing to deserve half of the farm. Sam's misplaced guilt and his misplaced trust had created this problem.

He stopped his thoughts. As his dad used to say, "Sufficient unto the day is the trouble thereof." For now he had to finish milking, then strain and refrigerate the milk, feed his cows, check for any new calves and try to get his big tractor going. He had to get the seed in the ground before that wet system that the weather forecaster kept predicting came rolling in.

He sent another squirt of milk toward the

kittens, enjoying the momentary distraction before he attended unto the trouble of this day and this week and the next six months.

Hannah strolled onto the yard and heard the muffled crow of a rooster breaking the early-morning quiet.

They really do that, she thought, following the sound. And all this time she thought it was just a clichéd sound effect added whenever a media person wanted to create a morning ambience.

Scout led her to a small, red barn where the noise was coming from. He stopped by the door and sat down, looking expectantly at her.

"You don't seriously think I'm going in there, do you?"

Scout tilted his head to one side.

"You can put that out of your mind right now. I'm no farmer and have no intention of becoming one."

Scout turned his head and lifted his ears as if he heard a noise, then trotted off across the yard toward a large red barn. Curious, Hannah followed him. As she came closer she heard Ethan's voice.

"On this farm you gotta pull your weight, right? You got to earn your keep. We got enough free-loaders on this farm right now," he continued. "Maybe I should call you Hannah."

Her face grew tight as Ethan's words registered. Freeloader. Taking more than you deserve.

She spun around and stalked away, her cheeks burning as her anger obliterated the soft feelings she'd just had toward him.

How dare he talk that way about her? What did he know? All his life he'd lived in the same place, had family around him. When he had stood at Sam's graveside, grieving, she was pretty sure he'd had a mother to put her arm around him, a father to support him.

She had stood by her mother's grave all alone.

He had family, a community, an entire support network.

Freeloader.

Pull your weight. Earn your keep.

Freeloader.

She shouldn't be surprised. She knew from the moment the conditions of the will had been read aloud how Ethan felt about her, but to hear him say it out loud had punctured her pride.

Hannah's feet hit the ground with muffled thuds as her anger consumed her. How dare he. She stopped halfway, then jumped as a figure sidled up to her.

Scout.

"What are you doing here?" she asked. "Shouldn't you be with your master? He won't appreciate your hanging around with a freeloader like me. My bad habits might rub off on you."

She heard it again. The crowing of the rooster.

And she had an idea. She could pull her weight on the farm. She might not know much, but she could watch and she could learn.

She walked over to the chicken barn, opened the door and pulled a face at the smell wafting out of the place. The startled rooster crowed, a few chickens flapped their wings and, in seconds, squawking chickens and feathers filled the air. Hannah pulled her head back as birds came at her. In a matter of minutes, the entire flock flew past her, squawking and flapping.

Hannah watched with dismay as the chickens, now free, ran to and fro, crowing and clucking and in general making enough noise to catch Ethan's attention.

And what was he going to say when he found out this city slicker had given his flock of chickens their freedom?

She may as well try to gather the eggs and find a way to corral the chickens later. She stepped inside the gloomy barn and there, to her right, was a row of boxes, raised off the ground. One chicken still sat inside a box, her eyes shut, looking quite content.

Hannah found two eggs in the first box, one of which was the same blue as the eggs that Ethan had brought her yesterday. Which presented her with her second problem. What to do with the eggs?

She looked around for a pail or a container, but

nothing. Ethan had brought them to the house in his hat, but she didn't wear a hat.

Oh well, into the pockets then. She would just have to be very careful.

The second, third and fourth boxes were devoid of eggs. Ethan had brought her almost a dozen eggs yesterday. Where could they be?

She approached the last box, guessing she had found the resting place of the rest of the eggs. The chicken inside didn't flick a feather, but turned her head and fixed her beady eyes on Hannah.

"I need to get your eggs," Hannah said, waving her hand at the chicken. Given how flighty the other ones were, she thought this was all she had to do to scare the hen off the nest. "Get out. Git. Shoo."

She drew a quick breath and slipped her hand underneath the chicken, who jabbed at her before Hannah even touched the eggs she was sure lay underneath her ruffled feathers.

Hannah jerked her hand back again and was about to retreat. But the thought of Ethan's words made her go after the eggs again, ignoring the chicken pecking frantically at her hand. She tried not to flinch as she pulled out two eggs, put them carefully in her pocket and went back for the rest.

The back of her hand was red, the chicken was squawking as if someone was murdering her, but as far as she could tell, she had gotten all the eggs.

She walked out of the gloomy barn into the warm sun feeling as if she had just conquered Everest. Scout was waiting for her and got up when she came near.

The rest of the chickens were pecking contentedly in the dirt when the chicken from the barn came screeching out of the door, clucking madly as if warning the rest about this madwoman who had stolen her precious eggs.

"Oh relax," Hannah said, patting her pockets to make sure the eggs were still safe. "You'll lay a bunch more tomorrow."

"Actually, she'll lay only one more tomorrow."

Hannah spun around, her cheeks flaming as Ethan sauntered toward her, carrying the pail of milk. He angled his chin toward her bulging pockets. "You gathered the eggs?"

The incredulous tone in his voice stung.

"Yes, I did." She bit back the words she really wanted to say. She didn't want him adding "eavesdropper" to the illustrious résumé entries "freeloader" and "mooch."

"I didn't think a city girl like you would want to go in the barn."

City girl. That one didn't sting as bad as the others, but his tone conveyed more than his words did.

"Well, some city girls," she said, laying heavy emphasis on the last word, "can be taught to…pitch in." She glanced at the pail of milk he carried. "Maybe I can even learn how to milk that cow."

The way his eyebrows shot up gave her a perverse sense of satisfaction. She would show him. Living on this farm was not her first choice. But she would prove to him that she could pull her weight, that she could, maybe in some small way, even be a benefit.

"I doubt it," he said.

Which made her all the more determined to try.

Chapter Seven

The next morning, gathering eggs went more smoothly, thanks to a few empty egg cartons she'd found.

She just had toast this morning for breakfast. No eggs. It would take her a while to sever the connection between the smell of the chicken barn, the feathers, the assorted…things on the floor of said chicken barn and the eggs that she was eating.

Ditto the milk.

Ethan had brought her a pail of milk this morning with instructions to let it sit so the cream could rise to the top. He would show her how to skim it off this afternoon, he said.

And now what? She could hardly stride out to where Ethan was working and demand that he teach her how to run a tractor or plant crops or work with cows. For now, she had to find her own way to contribute.

There was nothing to do in the house, so back outside she went. A faint breeze carried toward her the sounds of cows bellowing. When she went for a walk this morning, she had seen a bunch of them gathered in the corral, but they had been quiet.

Then she heard a tractor start up. Maybe Ethan was feeding them.

Scout had abandoned her for Ethan after she gathered the eggs this morning, so she was alone as she walked across the yard, following the noise of the cows and the tractor.

The bellowing of the cows grew louder and more insistent. Interspersed through their noise, she heard the higher-pitched bawl of calves. She got to the corral by skirting the barn, following the tire tracks of the tractor, which was now chugging through the herd of cows, holding aloft a large round bale of something. Hay? Straw?

Ethan drove the dusty green machine toward a long rectangle feeder and dropped the bale in with a muffled thud. He left the tractor running, got out and climbed into the feeder.

The cows were milling about, bawling. Suddenly a group of calves scurried around the tractor coming straight at Hannah, their tails up in the air. Then they saw her. They locked their feet and skidded to a halt, staring.

Most of them were completely brown, but two of them had blazingly white bellies and white splotches on their faces. They all had bright yellow tags hanging from their ears with numbers on them.

Hannah climbed the fence to get a better look. They jumped to the side, but then one of them took cautious, stiff-legged steps toward her, his head moving from side to side as if studying her, his large brown eyes unblinking.

"Aren't you guys just the cutest things," she said, smiling at the sight. The backs of the calves weren't much higher than her thighs, and as the one approached her, the others danced around, kicking up their heels.

The cows were occupied with Ethan and the tractor, so Hannah crouched down to make herself less imposing to the little animals.

The curious calf took a few more steps closer and Hannah held out her hand. The calf extended its head as far as it dared, its nostrils flaring as it tried to catch her scent.

"Its okay," she cooed.

The calf moved even closer, sniffing. And then, miraculously, its nose touched her extended fingers. Hannah couldn't stop smiling. What an adorable sight.

She moved just a little closer, trying to pet the calf. It jerked back with a throaty bawl of alarm.

"Oh, relax," Hannah scolded. "I'm not going to hurt you."

She tried to shuffle closer, but the calf, cautious now, let out another bawl, yet didn't run away.

"You don't have a name, do you?" Hannah said, angling her head to one side to read its ear tag. "So I'll just have to call you number fifty-five."

As she said the number aloud, something caught in the back of her mind. Fifty-five. Where had she heard that before?

Hannah heard another bawl, but this one was deeper, louder. She rose to see a large, snorting cow bearing down on her and the little calf.

And she remembered where she had heard that number.

The cow picked up speed, growing nearer by the second. Hannah glanced behind her, but the fence was about ten feet away. She took a quick step and tripped on a branch that she had avoided when trying to get near the calf.

Keep moving, her panicked mind shrieked as she stumbled and tried to gain her balance. She scrambled toward the fence, her hands scrabbling for purchase on the dusty ground, her feet pedaling. She caught the bottom rail of the fence and, though her entire focus was on getting away, she couldn't prevent another look over her shoulder.

The angry, bellowing cow was feet away, her eyes wide and bloodshot and focused on Hannah.

I'm not going to make it, Hannah thought, fear and adrenaline coursing through her as she grabbed for the next rail, trying to pull herself up and over the fence before she got squashed by the raging cow.

A sharp bark and a blur of brown and black distracted her for a split second. Another bark and the cow's attention was no longer on her, but on Scout, who was dancing between Hannah and the cow. Scout jumped toward the cow as if he was going to bite her nose. The cow lowered her head and charged at the dog, who shifted easily out of harm's way. Teasing, luring, Scout created room for Hannah. She scrambled over the fence and fell with an ignominious thud on the other side. As she lay on her back, she stared up at the sky, her heart thumping in her chest, her breath coming in gasps.

Swallowing a mouthful of grit, she pushed herself to her feet to see what was happening.

The cow was now licking her calf, making low, guttural noises that sounded curiously like consolation, assuring her baby that all was well. She looked up at Hannah, shook her head as if warning her off, and then she turned and ambled away, the calf bobbing alongside her.

Scout stood about ten feet away, his eyes fixed on the cow that plodded past him, paying him no attention whatsoever.

Hannah drew another trembling breath as Ethan drove the tractor alongside her. He hopped out and vaulted the fence, coming to land beside her.

"Are you okay? I saw what happened."

Hannah couldn't speak, so she simply nodded.

"I didn't know what was going on until Scout took off." He patted Scout, who had followed him through the fence. "Good dog, Scout. You saved the city girl."

Which had the effect of negating any warmth she might have felt at his concern. "He did and I'm grateful."

"I warned you about fifty-five, didn't I?" Ethan said, as if she should have remembered every tidbit of information he had tossed at an overwhelmed "city girl."

"You did. I forgot."

Ethan frowned at her. "You sure you're okay?" He took a step toward her and carefully lifted her hair away from her face. "You look like you hurt yourself here."

And why did her face tingle ever so slightly as his hands feathered over the tender spot on her cheek?

She jerked back, angry at her reaction. Especially considering that she knew exactly what he thought of her. To cover her reaction, she swiped at the dirt on the knees of her jeans. "This city girl is just fine," she said.

Ethan gave a light laugh. "Sorry. Bad habit. I

used to date a girl from the city. I called her that all the time."

"Which would explain the past tense of the dating experience," Hannah said. His freeloading comment of the other morning and his casual touch only seconds ago created a desire and need to create some distance between them.

"Actually, I broke up with her."

"Why am I not surprised?"

Ethan was looking at her curiously now, but she wasn't going to explain herself to him. She tested the arm she had landed on, guessing that it would be sore tomorrow morning.

She looked past him at the cows, some of which were now sticking their heads into the feeder, the other, less fortunate ones still waiting. Curiosity overcame her anger. "I thought cows ate grass."

"They'll be out on pasture in a few weeks. I like the grass in the pasture to get ahead of the cows before I put them out. Otherwise they'll chew it down too quick."

"I see." She didn't really, but she would learn. "So, how hard is it to run that tractor?"

"Not hard." She could see by his puzzled expression that he wasn't sure where she was going with this.

"Could you teach me?"

"And why do you want to learn?"

"If I'm going to be here six months, I figure I should learn how to do more than just gather eggs."

Ethan scratched his cheek with his forefinger, as if testing the idea. "I suppose I could teach you, though it's not a skill that translates well to the city."

"You never know when it might come in handy," she said with a sardonic tone.

"Okay, then. Come on over and I'll show you."

A few minutes later, Hannah was regretting her impulse. She had wedged herself between the driver's seat and a narrow ledge not built for sitting on while Ethan explained the various controls of the tractor. Her position was way too close to him. And what was worse, in spite of her anger with him, she couldn't help watching how his hands easily maneuvered the controls, how at home he was here in this tractor.

"These are your gears. In each gear you've got high and low. This is Reverse. Here's your Park brake, which you'll want to use when you're feeding cows. The last thing you want is your tractor running away on you while you're in the feeder cutting twine."

Ethan flicked through the gears, with the ease of one who knew intimately how and when to use each.

"So, how do you control that thing?" Hannah asked, trying to ignore the scent of grass intertwined with the hint of his cologne.

"That thing is your front-end loader. I've got the

bale forks on it now. They stab the bale and let you carry it around." Ethan pointed to a single knob mounted beside the gears. "You push up on this joystick to make it go down, down to make it go up, sideways to tilt it up or down."

Which made no sense at all to her.

"Do you want to sit with me while I get another bale?" Ethan asked, flicking a lever, releasing the clutch and backing away from the feeder.

Not really, but she had started down this road and she had to see it to the end. "Sure."

She watched his every move, trying to memorize what he used when, but the sight of his profile, softened now as he worked, was distracting her. This close she could see a fan of wrinkles at the corner of his eye, the glint of whiskers on his chin, the glow of his eye and the way his mouth curved up at the corner as he worked.

She had seen him tense, but he looked completely relaxed now. And too appealing.

You're just lonely, she reminded herself, concentrating on what he was telling her. He's the only person that you know here....

She made herself stop before she really started feeling sorry for herself.

"First rule of farm etiquette," he said as they neared the gate between the corrals and the rest of the yard. "Passengers in any vehicle always open and close the gates."

He tilted her a grin, which didn't help her determination to remain aloof.

Freeloader, she reminded herself as she pushed open the tractor door. He thinks you're a freeloader.

Hannah climbed carefully out of the cramped cab, trying not to let the size of the tires only inches away intimidate her. One roll of them and she'd be squashed like a bug.

Thankfully the gate was easy to operate and she swung it open as he drove through. Then she closed it behind him and latched it shut.

Ethan waited for her to get back in the tractor, closed the door and they were off.

"You passed the first test," he said as they roared along the yard toward a stack of bales. "You remembered to close the gate behind me."

"That was a test?"

Ethan laughed. "Trust me, I've dated a few girls who didn't catch on to the basic concept of gates and fences and their purpose vis-à-vis livestock."

"Did you just say vis-à-vis?" Hannah asked, preferring not to contemplate how many other women had done precisely what she was doing right now.

Ethan shrugged as he easily speared a bale with his forks and backed away from the pile. "I is edjumacated."

"Obviously," Hannah said drily. She watched as he shifted, adjusted, drove and maneuvered and then they were back at the gate.

They repeated the process two more times. "How much do these bally things eat?" she asked, while she rolled up the twines he tossed down at her from his perch atop the last bale.

"I'm giving them enough for a couple of days."

He jumped down off the feeder and landed in front of her. "So. That's how I feed the cows until they get out on pasture."

"And when will that happen?"

"Hopefully in the next couple of weeks. Once I get the crop in." Ethan took the rolled-up strings from her hand. "Your cheek looks sore yet," he said.

Oh, he was good, she conceded. Acting all concerned and caring in spite of how he felt about her. No wonder he had no shortage of women calling him.

"Yeah. It's okay."

"I think there's some medicated ointment in the medicine cabinet in the bathroom."

"Thanks. I'll take that under advisement."

"Advisement?" He lifted his eyebrows in a mocking gesture. "You is edjumacated, too?"

"Hannah can read," she said.

His eyes crinkled up as he laughed, hiding the faint white lines radiating from the corners of his eyes. Lines which meant he spent a lot of time outdoors, squinting as he worked in the sunshine.

Unlike Alex, whose face had been even smoother than hers. Hannah brushed aside the thoughts and memories. She hadn't thought about Alex for a while. No sense bringing up that old misery now.

But he did serve as a good reminder of how a man could mess up a life. If one let him.

Without a second look Ethan's way, she headed toward the house. She wanted to treat her cheek. She went directly to the bathroom and dug through the medicine cabinet looking for the salve Ethan had talked about. But all she found was an old squeezed-out tube of toothpaste, some disposable razors and four half-full pill bottles.

She pulled one down, glancing at the name.

Sam Westerveld.

Hannah clutched the pill bottle, as her jumbled emotions coalesced. The last picture she held in her mind was of Sam standing by the car, looking up at her as she stood behind the curtain of the apartment building. She remembered how her mother had pulled her away from the window and once again she wondered if any thought or remembrance of them had crept through his mind when he had come back here.

Hannah brushed the memories aside as she bent over to splash water on her face. She patted her cheeks dry, checked the scrape in the mirror once more. It would be okay.

The ringing of the phone sliced into the silence and Hannah jumped.

Relax, you ninny, she chided herself as she picked up the phone and said a breathless hello.

"Hi. Is Ethan there?" And yet another female asking for Ethan.

Hannah walked to the kitchen, tucked the phone under her ear and found the pad that already held the names and numbers of two different women who had called yesterday.

"Why don't you give me your name and number and I'll make sure he gets it." And maybe you'll have to take a number, as well.

"Tell him Jocelyn called. He's expecting my call." Hannah rolled her eyes at the brash assumption.

"I'll do that."

"And who are you?"

"Relative," she replied succinctly as she scribbled Jocelyn's name under the other two. The terse answer had worked with the other two girls so she'd decided to adopt it as her phone title.

The house was still clean so she went outside and made a quick tour of the yard around the house as she had promised herself she would when she was done inside.

Along the foundation of the house lay a flower bed, green shoots pushing through a tangle of old growth. Remnants of other plants edged the sidewalk. Behind the house, she found a small archway, also laden with woody stems. Tiny green buds were scattered over the old wood. The archway led to an area covered with paving stones and surrounded with more overgrown flower beds and what looked like a rock garden partially buried in leaves. A couple of wrought-iron chairs lay on their sides on the paved area, drawing her attention to a small pond in the center of the flat stones, its water covered with a scum of dead leaves. A small figure holding a pitcher sat poised above the pond as if pouring water into it.

Then she looked up and grew still. Another wooden trellis, about ten feet wide and topped with carved beams, framed the view of the lake beyond. Come summer this place would be a small piece of paradise, but it looked as if no one had done anything with it for a couple of years.

Her mind flashed back to Sam and the pots of flowers and tomatoes taking up most of the space on the tiny balcony of their apartment. A tiny oasis Hannah had often crouched down in, pretending she was hiding in a lush, soothing garden instead of overlooking a dingy parking lot and an equally dingy apartment building twenty feet away.

Sam had done this. She was convinced. And it looked as if Ethan had simply let it all go.

She pulled away the detritus of growth from previous years. Here, as in the front flower beds, shoots of green were pushing up through the ground, some already six inches high.

She pulled more branches and stems away,

tossing them onto the paving stones behind her, discovering more plants. Dirt gathered under her fingernails as she worked, but the excitement of her discoveries kept her on her knees, digging and cleaning.

Two hours later her knees ached; she had three broken fingernails, a kink in her back and a heap of sticks, leaves and branches piled up in the middle of the paving stones.

She slowly got to her feet, straightening her stiff knees as she smiled at the transformed garden. Removing the old growth had created space between the perennials to plant annuals. Hannah wondered if there was a greenhouse in town.

"Ethan should get you a wheelbarrow."

Hannah screamed, then whirled around, pressing her hand on her chest as if to keep her heart inside.

The woman walking toward her wore a huge sun hat and a loose dress in a bright shade of yellow. As she approached, she held out her hand. "Dot Westerveld. I'm Ethan's mom. I came to get some eggs from Ethan and thought I'd stop by and introduce myself."

Hannah pulled off her gloves and shook her hand, her heart still pounding.

"You've been busy," Dot said, her hands resting on her ample hips as she studied the yard. "Sam would be proud."

"Hey, Mom." Ethan came around the house, the dog trotting behind him. "I was wondering where you took off to. I got the eggs out of the trailer and put them in your car, like you asked."

"Just thought I'd say hi to Hannah before I left."

"You're leaving already?" Ethan asked.

"I want to get those eggs to Dodie and I have an appointment that I'm already late for." Dot laughed as if this was of minor consequence. "So I'll be going."

Hannah just nodded as Dot gave Ethan a quick kiss. "Take care of yourself, son. Thanks for the eggs." She flashed Hannah a broad smile. "Make sure my son gets you that wheelbarrow, okay?"

And as quickly as she came, she left.

Ethan watched his mother go, then turned to Hannah. "Sorry about the lightning visit. Mom comes and goes on her own schedule."

"Does she stop by more often?"

"Usually we meet in town, but I guess she wanted to see you."

Hannah didn't know what to say to that. She had always thought that the Westerveld family wasn't much interested in her. Scout pushed his nose into Hannah's hand and she stroked his head, feeling bemused.

"I'll get you a wheelbarrow." Ethan turned and started walking away, and Hannah had no choice but to follow.

As promised, Ethan brought her to a small shed. Inside, one wall had shelves filled with pots, small garden tools and coiled-up hoses. The other wall had rakes, shovels and hoes hanging neatly from nails. Everything she needed to work on the flower beds. At the end sat a wheelbarrow. "If you need anything else, I guess you can find it here."

Hannah simply nodded.

"You don't have to work that hard, you know," he said.

Hannah held his gaze. "Yes. I do."

Ethan said nothing but didn't look away, as if trying to find the meaning behind her words. "I guess it helps."

Now Hannah was puzzled. "What do you mean?"

"I just lost Sam. You just lost your mother. I know that keeping busy keeps me from falling into sadness. I'm sure it's the same for you."

The faint smile, the gentle tilt of one corner of his mouth and his lowered voice gently pried her own sorrow up from the place she had stored it tightly away.

"I never told you that I was sorry for your loss, as well," Ethan continued, tipping his head to one side, as if trying to see her from another angle. As if trying to understand her.

Hannah swallowed down an unexpected wave of sadness at his equally unexpected sympathy, looking down to hide her emotions.

And when he took a step nearer and gently laid a hand on her shoulder, she fought the urge to drift closer to him, to take the support and comfort he was offering.

She had to stop this or she was going to end up like those pathetic women who kept calling. She drew back, holding her head up. "I almost forgot to tell you that Jocelyn called."

"Yeah. So?"

"She said you were expecting her call."

"Okay."

She could see him trying to catch her eye, but though she avoided looking directly at him, she could see a smile crawl across his well-shaped lips. "Don't tell me you're jealous?"

The nerve. The absolute gall.

"You wish."

Ethan held his hands up in a gesture of surrender. "Just checking is all."

"Maybe you'd better go check on your tractor while I continue my freeloading."

Ethan's eyes narrowed as if he caught her meaning. She walked past him to get the wheelbarrow. Let him study on that for a while.

Chapter Eight

As Ethan walked up to his trailer, he spied the pail of freshly washed eggs sitting beside the metal step. Hannah had been busy.

After milking the cow this morning, he had stopped at the chicken house and checked the chicken feeder, but it looked as if Hannah had passed that test, as well.

Yesterday, after cleaning up the flower beds, she had taken out the lawn mower and the rototiller and, without asking his help, had managed to get them both going. Now the lawn was mowed and the overgrown garden worked up. His mother would be upset if she found out he hadn't helped Hannah. But what could he do if she didn't ask? It seemed she was determined to prove herself useful.

As if she was determined to prove she wasn't a freeloader. He'd wondered about her comment, then realized she must have overheard him. And now she was trying to prove him wrong.

At least he didn't have to worry about keeping her entertained. She seemed more than capable of handling herself.

For now, the next thing on his mind was a trip to town to the tractor dealership to get the parts that Derek had practically assured him on his mother's grave were exactly the parts he needed to get his big tractor going.

His cell phone rang and he snapped it open.

"Hello there," he said, surprised Hannah had called so quickly. "I'm just heading to town."

"Great, you can meet me there."

How had she gotten to town on her own? Then he recognized the voice, and his faint expectation disappeared.

"Hey, Jocelyn." How did she get his private cell-phone number? As far as he could remember he had never given it to her.

Ethan switched his cell phone to his other ear as he started his truck. He glanced around the yard, but couldn't see Hannah anywhere. He'd left a note for her in the house telling her that he was going to town. He was sure she would need a few things by now.

"Haven't heard from you for a while. What's been keeping you so busy?"

"The usual. Calving cows. Fixing equipment.

Trying to put the crop in." Which he'd been trying not to get too stressed about. He could practically hear the calendar pages flipping. He had a week to get in the canola and less than that for the wheat. If he didn't get his field tractor repaired soon, his chances of a much-needed bumper crop would deplete as fast as the moisture in the soil.

"And I'm sure your—what is she?—step-cousin is keeping you busy, as well?"

"She's no relative at all," he insisted. And where was she now? he wondered, looking around the yard one last time as he backed away from his trailer. If it wasn't for the pail of freshly washed eggs sitting outside his trailer door this morning, or the scent of her perfume in the house, he could be excused for thinking she'd flown the coop.

"So where can we meet in town?" Jocelyn was asking.

"Not sure I have time." He didn't feel like connecting with Jocelyn today. He had too much on his mind and her chatter could be annoying.

He stopped himself. Jocelyn was a lot of fun and he had gone out with her a few times. At one time her chatter had been appealing enough, so it wasn't her fault that she had assumed something more might come of their association.

"Call me when you get to town."

"I'll see how things play out," he said vaguely. Then he blinked as he saw a figure walking down the road, a backpack slung over his back. A hitch-hiker? Way out here? "Take care," he said absently, then clipped the phone shut as he came closer to the person, who turned, walking back-ward, holding out a thumb.

He shook his head as he came closer.

Hannah.

Ethan pulled to a halt beside her and pressed a button to open the passenger window. "You can't be serious," he said, grinning at her as he leaned one elbow on the steering wheel.

But she wasn't grinning back. "How else was I supposed to get to town?"

"All you had to do was ask."

"I didn't know you were going."

Ethan waved away a mosquito. "I'm going now. Hop in before the bugs invade."

But she didn't immediately jump in the truck, peering down the road as if hoping for a different ride.

"Trust me, Hannah, no one else is coming." He knew he was probably her least favorite person right now, but she had no other options.

He saw her shoulders lift, as if sighing, then she pulled open the door and got in. She rested her backpack on her lap.

"I stopped by the house to see if you needed anything from town," Ethan said as he started driving.

She only nodded. Looked like it was going to be a long, quiet trip to town. Ethan turned on the radio just as his cell phone rang. He glanced at the display. Jocelyn again. He ignored it and slipped the phone back in his pocket.

"I don't mind if you talk on your phone," Hannah said.

"That was just Jocelyn."

To his surprise, Hannah laughed. "Judging from the number of times she's called the house, I would have guessed she rated more than a 'just.' Of course, what with the Alana calls interspersed with the Nancy and Pearl calls, I'm sure you have a hard time keeping track."

"Hey, I don't ask them to call me. I don't go running after women. Ever."

"You don't have to," she retorted. "They come running to you."

"Only some." He thought of Colby, who had run in the other direction. A woman who didn't want to be on the farm.

Ironic that now he was stuck with someone who wasn't interested in him and, thanks to overhearing a chance, uncensored comment, felt she had to contribute to the working of the farm. Trouble was, all she had to do was sit on a chair on the porch for six months and she would get half of what he and Sam had worked hard to get together.

He pushed back another, all too familiar, beat

of bitterness. He had to learn to cope, to find a way around this problem. Once he got the crop in he would double-check with Scholte to see how things were coming along with his contesting of the will.

"When we get to town, where do you want to go?" Ethan asked.

"I need some groceries and some seeds."

"Seeds? For what?"

"I was thinking that fresh vegetables would be nice come July or August or whenever it is that one expects vegetables from the garden."

Did she really figure on being around that long? Would Jace Scholte have everything settled by then? Knowing the glacial pace of lawyers when they were on the clock, he doubted it.

"Sam planted one all the time," he said. "He loved working in it. Except the past few years when he was sick."

Hannah fidgeted with the buckles on her backpack, then he saw a slow smile soften the harsh planes of her face. "When he lived with us he used to fill pots with tomatoes and flowers. He put them on the balcony. I remember how good those tomatoes tasted."

Because of Sam's inappropriate relationship with Hannah's mother, Ethan had avoided imagining Sam in that setting.

Yet Hannah, an innocent bystander to the relationship, would have her own memories and her own Sam stories.

"How long did he live with you and your mom?"

"I was young when they started dating. I think he moved in when I was six." She shrugged, her expression growing somber. "It seemed pretty normal to me at the time."

"What was he like when he lived with you?" he asked, seizing on the only thing they had in common.

"He was sweet. Soft-spoken. He used to walk me to school."

"Where did you live?"

"Scarborough. Just a few blocks from the GO train."

Ethan had no idea what she was talking about. "I thought you lived in Toronto."

"No, Sam always said that," Hannah replied. "He could never figure out the boundaries of the different suburbs of metro Toronto."

"What did he do there?"

"Odd jobs when he could. Mostly he worked as the janitor of the apartment block we lived in. I would help him most of the time when Mom…when I was bored."

"He can't have made much money doing that."

Hannah shrugged. "I wouldn't know. We always managed."

Of course they had. Ethan thought of the

money his grandfather had regularly sent to Sam and Hannah's mother. Money the farm badly could have used.

"I remember he used to take me for long walks on the days that—" Hannah stopped abruptly.

"On the days that…" Ethan prompted, curious as to why she stopped, as she had before.

"Nothing."

And thus ended another scintillating conversation with the continually elusive Hannah. Guessing she wasn't going to say much more, Ethan leaned over and hit the on button of the radio. The strains of classic rock filled the cab, Sam's favorite station. Four songs later they were on the edge of Riverbend and Ethan slowed down. "Where do you want me to take you?"

"I just need some groceries and then maybe you can tell me where I can buy some tomato plants?"

"I'll drop you off at the Riverbend Co-op. There's a seasonal garden section in the Farm and Feed building just past the bulk gas pumps. You can get everything you need there."

"Do they seriously call it the Farm and Feed?" she asked with a lilt of humor in her voice. "I always thought Sam was making a joke at my expense when he talked about that."

"No joke. That's the name." He slowed down and made a right turn. "And there's the proof." He turned into the parking lot of the co-op and pointed to the building with the incriminating words emblazoned on the side in three-foot-high neon letters. Ethan stopped. "We should arrange to meet somewhere when you're done."

"I can thumb a ride back."

"You saw how little traffic comes down our road, so you know how hard it will be to get a ride home." He pulled out his cell phone and handed it to her. "Here. Call Janie's place when you're done. I'll meet you there."

Hannah studied his phone as if it were a snake and shook her head. "I'll be okay."

Ethan sighed, leaned over farther and took her hand from where it rested on the dashboard of the truck. He pressed the phone into her palm and closed her fingers over top. "My mother would kill me if she found out that I let you hitchhike. The number is in the directory under Janie. I'll be there in half an hour. Call me."

Hannah jerked her hand back but kept the phone. "Okay, okay. I don't want you to get into trouble with your mother." She pocketed the phone, then, to his surprise, gave him an arch look. "Do you want me to take messages?"

Ethan frowned. "From who?"

Hannah ticked the names off on her fingers. "Jocelyn, Alana, Pearl and Nancy?"

His neck grew warm. She made him sound like a philandering creep. "Just tell them I'm busy."

Hannah's look morphed into a sly grin. "I'm sure they'd love to hear that from another woman."

"Hey, I don't go chasing after them," he protested. "That's not my style."

Hannah's eyes held his. "I suppose not," she said quietly, but she didn't look away. And neither did he.

As the moment lengthened, Ethan felt a gentle shift in his perceptions. He thought of the memories she had shared with him and tried to imagine her as a young girl living with Sam and her mother.

"Before you go, I should give you some money for groceries." He shifted to one side so he could pull his wallet out of his back pocket.

"I can pick up whatever you want and you can pay me back when we connect again."

Ethan pulled out a bunch of bills as he shook his head. "For you. I meant for you. Make sure you buy enough for a couple of weeks, though. I don't get to town much during harvest."

Hannah stepped out of the truck so fast Ethan thought she was going to fall. "I can pay for my own groceries, thanks," she said curtly.

"Well, I was just…"

"I'm not a mooch, okay? I pay my own way." She slammed the door shut and stalked away, her head high, her thick wavy hair flowing like a flag behind her, shining in the sun.

Ethan shoved his wallet back in his pocket,

angry at her response. He was just trying to be helpful. She didn't need to throw words back at him that she wasn't even supposed to have heard.

He drove off to the tractor dealership, storing thoughts of Hannah away in the "troublesome women" compartment of his life and focused on getting his tractor fixed.

There was more to life than tomato plants, Hannah thought, standing in front of the seed rack located in the greenhouse section of the Riverbend Farm and Feed.

Peaches and cream, sweet corn, early corn, late corn.

Imperator, Nantes, Danvers, Chatenay carrots.

Pole beans, broad beans, green beans, wax beans. Beets, zucchini, peas and over ten different varieties of lettuce.

Confusion fought with the urge to grab one of each type of seed as the possibilities of the sheer variety of vegetables that she could put in the garden expanded with every choice available to her. And at $1.50 per packet, the choices were cheap enough.

And then there were the flowers, the bright pictures on the envelopes promising a bounty of color.

The plant packets were portable enough. She could buy any number of them and carry them in her bag. But according to the greenhouse lady, if she wanted to eat ripe tomatoes by August, she would have to buy them as bedding plants and how was she supposed to carry those in her backpack and juggle her groceries, as well? She had done as Ethan had suggested and made sure she bought enough for a while. Her backpack was full.

The scent of rich earth and plants wafted from the open door of the greenhouse just beyond the seed racks, enticing her to come in and partake of the bounty that awaited her there.

How many packets should she get? Probably one would be more than enough. But she'd need some flowers to fill in the spaces between the perennials in Sam's garden. She pulled packets off the rack, reading the instructions, looking at the pictures and imagining where she could put each. A bubble of happiness lifted inside her as she thought of the flower garden and how it would look with delphiniums and hollyhocks in the back. In front of them she could plant daisies. They would come up fast. And these orange pansies.

She picked and planned, anticipation growing with the possibilities. And what about some petunias?

"…apparently he's living in the holiday trailer and she's in the house."

"I can't believe Sam would do that to his own nephew."

Hannah's hand paused midpluck as the voices drifted out of the greenhouse just beyond her. She swallowed, realizing they were talking about her.

She slipped the packet back, determined to walk away, but it was as if her feet remained rooted while her hearing became hypersensitive. She heard the rustle of the one lady's bag, the clip of her feet on the wooden floor of the greenhouse.

"Bad enough that he was getting money while he was there. The moneygrubbing didn't quit when Sam came back." The voice held a sharp edge of disdain.

"You can't know that for sure," the other woman replied.

"Ethan told me. That woman's family bled the farm for forever. Even after Sam finally listened to us and came to his senses and came back home, that didn't change."

Hannah finally placed the one voice. Tilly Westerveld. The other she didn't know at all. What money were they talking about? What had Ethan told his aunt?

"I'm just hoping she discovers that farm life isn't as easy as she thinks it is and leaves before the six months are over. Ethan has put so much into that farm it would be a shame if she just up and takes half...." The voices faded away. Hannah breathed in, trying to resurrect her previous emotions, but joy had been leached out of the afternoon. She stared at her seed packets lying in the bottom of the shopping basket and reached down to start putting them back.

That family. *Bled* the farm. These harsh comments dovetailed into what she had overheard Ethan say when he milked the cow.

How dare they judge her and her mother? How dare they imply that she had anything to do with Sam's will, she thought as she shoved the packets back in the racks.

She hadn't wanted this stupid farm, but circumstances had pushed her here and, as she had always had to most of her life, she adjusted. She made do. She coped.

Bled the farm. What could they have been talking about? She and her mother never took a penny from the farm.

She remembered Sam and her mother arguing about money, remembered her mother telling Sam that they needed more. She had always thought her mother was urging Sam to work harder.

Doubts flickered and grew in the face of Tilly Westerveld's certainty. As the harsh words echoed through her mind, she fumbled and dropped a package. When she bent over to pick it up, she was dismayed to feel the prickle of tears warm her eyelids. They were wrong. Had to be.

She pressed her hands to her face, took a deep breath and looked down at the seed packet. She had been so excited about planting a garden, but now it seemed like a waste of her time.

And what else are you going to do? Sit around and watch television and really be a freeloader?

No. She was going to do what she wanted to do and right now—she wanted to be true to Sam's legacy. She wanted to plant the garden that Sam had always planted.

And she was going to look for proof that Tilly was wrong.

She pulled the seed packets down again, tossing in a few of the flower seeds for good measure, then marched into the greenhouse. She was going to get her tomatoes and maybe a few other plants besides. Somehow she was going to pack them to the coffee shop in town and she was going take them back to the farm, *her* farm, and plant them.

However temporary they might be, she was putting roots down. She was going to stake her claim on a place no one thought she deserved.

And she was going to make sure no one had any cause to accuse her of being a freeloader. Ever.

The cashier rang up her purchases and the very helpful greenhouse lady rigged up a carrier for her to transport her seedlings. The seeds went into her backpack along with the groceries she had purchased.

If it weren't for the fact that she was rather

overloaded with purchases, she would have marched directly to the highway, stuck out her thumb and taken her chances.

But she had to be practical and Ethan wouldn't be happy with her. Besides, she still had his cell phone. And though he had asked her to call him at Janie's coffee shop, she preferred to make it there on her own. So she started walking.

The town was bigger than she realized, she discovered as she turned one more corner after asking directions from another helpful resident. As well, the day had warmed up. By the time she got to the coffee shop, she was hot, sweaty and her anger with Tilly and the Westerveld clan had morphed into plain, ordinary irritation.

Thank goodness the interior of the shop was pleasantly cool and welcoming with brightly colored tiles, curtains at the window and cheery prints on the wall.

Ethan wasn't there when she arrived, so she found an empty table, set her purchases on the floor and went to the counter to get something to drink.

"Hi, there. What can I get for you today? Something cool?" The dark-haired young woman behind the counter smiled pleasantly at her as she wiped off the counter. Hannah recognized her from the Saturday she had whiled away some time here while her partner, Lizzie, was stabbing her in the back out in Toronto.

"An iced cappuccino, please," Hannah said, digging in her purse for loose change.

"Good choice. You get your caffeine and your ice all in one tidy package. Plus, my iced cappuccino is the best in town."

"It's the only one in town, Janie," a man said as he walked up to the counter. Hannah gave him a cursory glance.

He was tall, with longish brown hair and a scar pulling down one side of his mouth that, combined with his teasing hazel eyes, gave him a sardonic look at odds with the neatly tailored gray suit, gray shirt and burgundy tie.

"It's the only one in town because I've scared off all the competition, Jace."

Hannah felt the man's eyes on her, but she wasn't going to look at him again. His tailored, tidy look reminded her of her ex-boyfriend, Alex, and that was reason enough to ignore him.

But the man would not be deterred. "I don't believe I've met you before," Jace was saying, still watching her.

"I don't believe you have, either," Hannah muttered, counting out her change as she laid it on the counter.

"My name is Jace Scholte. And you are…" His cultured voice raised the question and Hannah sighed.

"Not interested," she said curtly, pushing the

change across the counter to Janie. "I think that should cover it."

Hannah scooped up the rest of her loose change, dropping it into the plastic bin beside the till that bore a notice stating that the money would send some unfortunate child to camp.

"Generous and attractive," Jace was saying. Gracious, this guy just didn't quit.

"Honestly, Jace, you need to return that book on pickup lines to the library and find a more current one," Janie said above the whirring of the cappuccino machine.

"I don't know. I thought I was doing okay," he said, leaning an elbow on the counter, as if trying to get another angle on Hannah. "What do you think?"

"I try not to," Hannah said. "Makes my brain hot."

"Hence the iced cappuccino."

"Hence." Hannah looked at him then, trying to find a way to get rid of him. "Only lawyers use words like *hence*."

Jace raised his hands in a gesture of surrender. "Guilty as charged, Your Honor."

"Leave the girl alone, Jace. She's not from around here."

Had her bad manners given her away totally? "Does it show?"

"Sorry. I know that you're Hannah Kristoferson and that you're from Toronto." She handed Hannah her cappuccino with an apologetic smile at Hannah's surprise. "That's the way things go here in Riverbend. I can keep a secret—the people I tell it to can't."

The woman's good humor eased Hannah's own pique but seemed to have the opposite effect on Jace.

"So you're Hannah Kristoferson," he said, pulling away as if she had suddenly been diagnosed with chicken pox.

"Guilty as charged," Hannah shot back, puzzled at the sudden change in his attitude. Maybe he knew all about Hannah's "freeloading" ways, as well, or maybe he had overseen some of the "bleeding" she was supposed to have done.

The bell above the door tinkled and, in her peripheral vision, Hannah saw Ethan come into the shop.

"Just couldn't wait to make a move, could you, Jace?" Ethan was saying.

"My mama didn't raise no slowpoke," Jace said, but Hannah could hear that he was simply going through the motions now.

"Get you anything, Ethan?" Janie asked.

"Sure, cuz. I'll have what she's having."

Cuz. Was there anyplace in Riverbend where she wasn't going to bump up against a Westerveld or a relative of a Westerveld or the friend of a Westerveld?

"You look grumpy, Ethan. Bad day?" Janie asked

as Hannah returned to the table she had claimed, pulling away from this family and their attitude.

"The usual baloney. Wrong parts, so they're going to jerry-rig it. I have to pick that up in a bit."

The bell tinkled again and a pregnant blond woman accompanied by a dark-haired man came in. Sarah and Logan, Hannah overheard as she settled in at the table, resting her cappuccino in front of her. More cousins of Ethan's.

Hannah set aside her cappuccino, then pulled out a few packets of the seeds she had bought, trying to ignore the chatter of the people by the counter. They obviously belonged here, fit in.

Hannah wasn't the kind of person to feel sorry for herself. She had found out the hard way that no one joined in on a self-imposed pity party, but her ego had taken a beating back there at the greenhouse and she didn't think she could be blamed for feeling funky right now.

Seeing Ethan surrounded by family, laughing and joking around didn't lessen the funk. He belonged, she didn't.

And when Tilly Westerveld came into the shop as well she figured she'd reached maximum levels of tolerance.

That is, until the entire troupe, minus Jace the lawyer, followed Ethan to her table.

"Hello, Hannah, how are you doing?" the girl named Sarah asked as she set her coffee on the table and then pulled a chair closer. "Going to try to plant a garden?" she asked, pointing to the seed packets Hannah still had laid out in front of her.

"*Try* being the operative word," Hannah said, her tone polite but distant. She wondered what this particular Westerveld thought of her. Not that she cared, but it would help to know just so she didn't make any kind of conversational faux pas.

As Hannah gathered up the packets, she shot a quick glance at Tilly Westerveld, but Tilly was chatting with Ethan as she sat down across from Hannah. To Hannah's dismay, Ethan settled himself beside Hannah.

"Logan, I don't know if you've met Hannah." Sarah turned to the dark-haired man who was dragging another chair to the table. "She's staying on Grandpa's farm for the next half year."

Sarah's diplomatic wording of the awkward situation was a surprise to Hannah. And a pleasant switch from what she'd undergone with Tilly and Ethan.

"Hannah, this is my husband, Logan Carleton." Logan made appropriate noises and shook her hand then sat back, seemingly content to simply watch and listen.

"How are you managing?" Sarah asked Hannah.

Hannah was about to reply when Sarah arched her back, pressing the flat of her hand against her stomach.

"You okay, Sarah?" Logan asked, his voice gruff but his hand gentle on her shoulder.

"Baby just moved."

"When are you due?" Hannah asked.

"Six weeks...four weeks..." Logan and Sarah answered at once.

"So who's right?" Ethan asked, breaking into the conversation.

"I am," they both replied.

Laughter followed the comments and the conversation ebbed and flowed as topics ping-ponged back and forth between the participants. Hannah, captive in her corner, was relegated to spectator.

Tilly glanced her way once in a while and every time she did, her eyes seemed to hold a glimmer of reproach. Hannah chose to ignore her.

The door jangled open again, letting in a tall, slender woman. She waved at Janie behind the counter and headed directly toward the table where the Westervelds sat. She had short blond hair, feathered to frame her face and streaked with pink and green highlights. Pink crystals hung from her ears, matching the pink tank top she wore.

"Hey, family," she said, waving inch-long purple nails at everyone at the table.

"Hey, Dodie, did the Care Bears survive the collision with you?" Ethan asked, adding a grin.

"It's my pastel phase," she said, fluttering her overly made-up eyes at him.

Then, to Hannah's surprise and amazement, she walked over to Tilly's side, bent over and brushed her cheek with a kiss. "Hey, Mom."

"Dorothea, how are you?"

Hannah watched, trying to make a connection between the psychedelic wonder that was Dodie, or Dorothea as her mother called her.

"I'm doing great," she said with enthusiasm. She glanced over at Hannah, then reached past Tilly, holding her hand out. "Hey. I'm Dodie. You Ethan's latest?"

Hannah was about to protest when Ethan said, "Hannah, this specimen of poor taste is my cousin Dodie. She spends her time trying to get the good citizens of Riverbend to part with their money by way of her consignment store and parking her sweet self at the Farmers Market. Dodie, this is Hannah Kristoferson. She's staying at the farm."

Hannah waited for the inevitable shift in her welcoming expression at the introduction but Dodie just nodded. "Cool. You don't mind being parked way out there?"

"It has its challenges," Hannah said, catching Tilly's quick glance.

"Dodie, you going to order some coffee or are you just going to hang around and harass my customers?" Janie asked, joining the group.

"Just a will o' the wisp, passing through," Dodie said. "I was on my way to Preston to pick up a consignment of clothes and saw you all gathered and thought I would pay my familial respects." She patted her mother on the shoulder, as if underlining her mission.

In the general chatter that followed, Janie turned to Hannah.

"How are you managing way out in the boonies?" Janie asked. "You don't have a vehicle, do you?"

"No, I don't," Hannah admitted. "I got a ride from Ethan this morning."

"You ever need to get to town, call me," Dodie said. "Don't wait for this yahoo to bring you in." She threw Ethan another annoyed look. "He only comes to town if he's bored or needs a part or some woman has decided that she simply can't live without him."

"What's with the switching allegiances?" Ethan protested. "I thought I was your cousin. Your best friend."

"I'm a woman first. And when it comes to hapless men, we women need to help each other out." Dodie grinned at Hannah. "If you get lonely, call me. I'm on the road a lot."

"Thanks for the invitation," she said. "I might take you up on that."

"You make sure you do. Now tell me, what kind of seeds did you buy?"

Hannah pulled them out. Janie came to look over her shoulder and soon Dodie, Sarah and Janie were giving her advice and suggestions. Janie offered to come and help her put the garden in, but Hannah said she'd manage.

"Just make sure you remember what you planted where," Janie advised.

"Or you could just scatter the seed and let gardening become an adventure," Ethan put in, joining the conversation.

"Says Mr. Control Freak himself," Janie scoffed.

"You should talk, Mrs. I-can't-live-without-my-agenda."

"I have three kids and a business. My agenda is my lifeline. You, however, in spite of being single, have never done anything spontaneous or unplanned in your life. You have your PDA with you everywhere you go." As if to underline her point, Janie reached over and pulled said PDA out of Ethan's shirt pocket.

"Aha," she said, waving it aloft. "Let's see who he has in his little electronic black book." Janie flipped open the leather cover and sent a wink Ethan's way. "Whoa, that's a lot of listings. My goodness, pictures even." Janie lowered the device and shook her head. "Ethan, Ethan. Pearl?" She sighed.

"Janie…" Ethan's voice was serious now as he held out his hand. "Don't make me hurt you."

"Idle threats." Janie bent down and brought the PDA down to Hannah's level, showing her a picture of a sultry-looking blonde with pouting lips that glistened and half-shut eyes that spelled out an invitation that most men would RSVP to immediately. "I ask you, Hannah, as a nonmember of the Westerveld family and probably a good judge of character, does this look like potential wife material?"

Before Hannah could reply, Ethan plucked the PDA out of Janie's hands. He wasn't smiling anymore. "I don't need a wife. I need my cousins to stay out of my life."

"You know, Hannah, we try." Janie sighed. "We give the young man dating advice. We try to set him up with good Christian women who will make good wives. And what does he do? Date Miss Sweet But Incompatible and then accuse us of interfering."

"Classic male defense mechanism," Sarah said dryly. "Not to mention self-sabotage. Date a girl you know your family would never approve of and you have a built-in reason to avoid proposing."

Ethan tucked the PDA into his shirt pocket and sent his cousins a world-weary glance. "You finished dissecting my love life?"

"What love life?" they said in unison, as if this conversation covered well-traveled ground.

Hannah smiled as she thought of the list of names on the message pad by the phone. As for Ethan, he looked as if someone had just dumped salt packets in his drink. "Logan, you going to help me out?"

Logan's only support was to send him a lazy smile. "Your reputation precedes you, Ethan."

"You girls shouldn't tease," Tilly Westerveld said, sending a comforting smile Ethan's way. "Ethan hasn't had it easy, either. I'm sure he still thinks about—"

"Not going there, Aunt Tilly." Ethan cut her off so fast Hannah wondered what she was going to say. "As for the rest of you, Hannah doesn't need to know *all* my secrets."

In spite of Ethan's smile, Hannah caught the faintest shadow of something indefinable in his eyes. Sorrow?

What was his history and what was the little secret he alluded to?

"Hannah, are you about done your cappuccino?" Ethan asked, looking at his watch. "I need to pick up that part and get my tractor fixed before harvest season."

"What's your rush?" Janie asked. "We haven't even started asking Hannah all the fun questions yet."

Now it was *really* time to go, Hannah thought. From the way Janie, Sarah and Dodie had gone for Ethan, she guessed that their idea of fun questions were ones she wouldn't want to answer, either.

"I'm ready," she said. She gathered up her seed

packets, tucked them into her knapsack and lifted up the tray of tomato plants she had sitting on the floor.

"Bedding plants, too? You are adventurous," Janie said, standing aside so Hannah could maneuver past her.

"Were you at the greenhouse?" Tilly asked, her eyes narrowing.

Was she remembering her conversation there? "Yes, the one at the Farm and Feed." She looked directly at Tilly.

But Tilly held her gaze as if meeting her challenge. "They've got good plants there," she said simply.

Chapter Nine

~⚞~

Was that a tractor running?

Ethan sat up in his bed, listening to the unmistakable putt-putt of his John Deere.

Puzzled, he glanced at the blinking zeroes on his bedside alarm clock. The power must have gone off last night.

The angle of the sun slanting into the trailer registered.

Rats. He'd slept in. And someone was trying to steal one of his tractors.

He yanked on his pants and grabbed his shirt as he slipped bare feet into his battered cowboy boots. No time for socks. He had to get outside and find out what was going on. He shouldn't have let Scout sleep in the house with Hannah. The dog would have warned him about the intruder.

Ethan snapped the buttons on his shirt as he

jogged across the yard, trying to pinpoint the sound. There. In the corrals.

Surely a potential thief wouldn't be running the tractor in the corrals? He ran around the corner of the barn and skidded to a halt.

Scout was trotting alongside the tractor, like he always did when Ethan fed the cows and, at the wheel, Ethan caught the unmistakable outline of Hannah's abundant hair. The bale forks held a bale of hay and she was driving the tractor toward the feeder.

How in the world had she figured out so quickly how to run the tractor, let alone handle the front-end loader? He only remembered giving her the one lesson. This was not going to turn out well.

The tractor slowed down, then jumped ahead, the bale on the forks bouncing.

Fearful for his tractor's transmission in the hands of this rank amateur, Ethan vaulted over the fence and ran toward the vehicle.

She stopped the tractor, then it slowly crawled ahead. Ethan easily caught up but waited until she stopped by the feeder before he dared get into the cab.

He clambered up the steps and yanked the door open.

"What do you think you're doing?" he shouted above the noise of the engine.

She ignored him as she studied the controls for

the loader. "Up is down and down is up," he barely heard her mutter over the noise of the cows and the tractor.

"Stop right now," he ordered. "You don't know what you're doing."

She turned to him and he already knew her well enough to recognize the set of her jaw and the determination in her eyes. "I'm learning."

"At the expense of my tractor."

"I haven't stalled it yet." She raised the loader, inched the tractor ahead then pushed the joystick to one side. The bale tipped down, then with agonizing slowness slipped off the forks into the feeder. She gave Ethan a smug look. "You going to get out of my way so I can cut strings?"

"Hannah, I don't know what you're trying to prove, but I'll feed the cows."

Hannah made a show of glancing at her watch. "You snooze, you lose. Besides, weren't you supposed to be up bright and early this morning, getting your crop in?"

"The power went out last night. I slept in."

"I'm not surprised. You must have been up until midnight working on that tractor."

He wondered how she knew.

"So, why don't you go get that monster tractor of yours going and go plant your wheat or barley or whatever it is you plan on sticking in the ground and let me finish up here," she said, getting up from the seat, which ended up putting her close enough to him that he caught the faintest hint of vanilla from her hair.

He hadn't moved yet and found he didn't want to move.

Their eyes met and once again he felt it. That frisson of attraction that was at once familiar and yet not. He clenched his fists to keep himself from reaching up and brushing that errant strand of hair out of her face.

He was attracted to her. That much was inarguable. He'd been attracted to any number of women since Colby, but always in an abstract way. Like one would appreciate a painting.

But Hannah brought up a mixture of emotions in him he hadn't been able to pin down. Attraction, yes. Annoyance, double yes. But something else.

She didn't encourage him in any way, shape or form. In fact, around him she often acted as if she would have preferred him completely out of her life.

Maybe that was it, he thought as he wordlessly stood aside so she could squeeze past him, that smell of vanilla growing stronger, her hair brushing his face as she passed. Maybe she held an extra appeal because she seemed so elusive.

Ethan clung to that. Had to if he was going to spend six months with this woman underfoot. Once she was gone…

Trying to bring that thought to completion was

enough to extinguish any foolish romantic notions he might be harboring for this woman. Once she was gone, so was half the farm.

He watched as she clambered up and over the metal bars of the large feeder then struggled to cut the strings. He should go help her or, if not, at least show her how to do it.

Stifling a sigh, he got out of the tractor and climbed into the feeder behind Hannah.

"It works easier if you cut the strings way down on the bottom of the bale," he said, pulling out his jackknife and showing her how it was done. "Then, when you go to the other side and pull the strings loose, you don't have to pull such a long string."

Hannah watched, silent as he showed her how.

"Why are you doing this?" he asked as he handed her the jackknife.

"I'm doing this because I know how busy you are and I want to help."

He felt a peculiar warmth at her pronouncement.

"I'm going to be here a while," she continued, "and there's no way I'm going to sit around every day. If I'm going to have half this farm, then I want to say I deserve to have half."

And the warmth dissipated in the cold reality of their situation.

"Okay. Suit yourself," Ethan said, tucking his shirt in his pants. "I usually give the cows three bales in this feeder and two in the other. You'll have to keep an eye on how much they're eating. I feed them every three days, but it looks like they've been eating more lately."

"I know. I heard them bawling last night and I saw a bunch of them hanging around the empty feeder."

Observant as well as good-looking.

"In a couple of weeks, they'll be out on pasture," Ethan continued. "I've got a few more cows to calve, as well, so I'll be busy with them for a bit." Ethan pulled off the rest of the strings from the bale and held his hand out for the ones that Hannah had pulled off. "I can finish this up...."

Hannah shook her head. "No way. I always finish what I start. Always."

She clambered out of the feeder, Ethan right behind her. Before she got into the tractor, Ethan touched her arm to get her attention.

"Get the next two bales from the north stack," he told her when she turned around. "That's better hay."

Hannah looked up at the sun as if judging its position, glanced over her shoulder at the stacked-up bales of hay, then nodded.

"And watch the brakes, they're a bit touchy at times."

"I found that out," she said, giving him a self-conscious smile.

"You sure you're okay with running this

tractor?" he asked again. He couldn't imagine how she had caught on so quickly.

"If you trust me with it?"

What could he say? Sam and Ethan had bought the tractor together. If she was now part-owner of the farm, half of this selfsame tractor was hers.

"I'll have to, won't I?" he said, stepping away.

"I'll be careful," she promised. Then she stepped into the tractor, closed the door and smoothly reversed away from the feeder. Looked like she knew what she was doing, he had to admit.

So he followed her out of the corrals, one eye out for 55 and her calf, then he closed the gate behind Hannah and latched it.

He waited a moment, watching as Hannah approached the bales and slowly lowered the loader. It took her a few tries, but she managed to stab the bale. A few more tries got it tipped back so it wouldn't slide off the forks and then she was turning around.

She caught on quick, he gave her that.

As he jogged back to his trailer, he thought of the convenience of having her feed the cows for the next few weeks. That would free up time for him to get into the field at the crack of dawn.

For the first time since the reading of Sam's will, the tension gripping Ethan's neck eased off.

This could work okay, he thought as he stepped into his trailer to pack up his lunch.

* * *

The sun-warmed earth squeezed between her toes as Hannah raked the dirt over the last row of bean seeds she had just dropped into the ground. She had taken off her shoes and socks, relishing the feel of the dirt on her bare feet.

"Do you want me to tamp the row?"

Dodie stood at one end of the row with a large flat board attached to a long metal handle. The "tamper" she had told Hannah about when she showed up at the garden this morning.

When Hannah had come in from the long process of feeding the cows she had checked the messages on the answering machine. Three for Ethan—no surprises there—and—surprise—one for her. Dodie. She was coming to pick up eggs. And when she arrived and found Hannah in the garden, she threw off the patchwork vest she was wearing, rolled up the cuffs of her capris and dug in, ignoring Hannah's protests.

At first Hannah had felt awkward putting in a garden in Sam's plot with the help of Sam's niece. Dodie, after all, belonged here. But Dodie was full of stories and talked about Sam without a trace of discomfort. She was easy company, and as they worked, managed to weasel some of Hannah's own stories out of her. Hannah had resisted at first, but Dodie made her laugh and, more importantly, made her feel as if she could be completely herself without judgment. So she told her about her thwarted plans and about Lizzie.

"So this girl completely cut you out? What a rat." Dodie banged the tamper on the ground with more force than necessary.

"So that's one of the reasons I decided to stay here," Hannah said, brushing the dirt off her knees as she stood up.

"Don't blame you." Her reply surprised Hannah and, at the same time, gently condoned Hannah's choice. "Did you mark the row?"

"Doing it now." Hannah stuck the empty seed packet on a stick.

"Why don't you water those tomato plants and I'll finish up here," Dodie said, tamping down on the last row of seeds.

"How long before I see anything coming up?" Hannah cleaned up the leftover bits of packaging and sticks used to mark the rows.

"Shouldn't take more than three, four days for the onion sets, the rest, about a week, tops."

"Thanks for helping me. Do you want to come up to the house for some juice?"

"Sounds good." They cleaned up the garden tools and put them back in the shed beside the garden.

But before they left, Hannah looked out over the packed ground with its neatly marked rows. A pair of swallows dove over the garden, the sun flashing on their iridescent wings. A light breeze teased the warmth of the sun away from her flushed skin as she wiggled her toes in the warm dirt and a gentle sigh of contentment eased out of her.

"This is really a day of firsts for me," she said. "First time I've planted a garden anywhere but in a pot, first time I fed cows."

"Ethan made you feed the cows?"

"That wasn't Ethan's idea. I took the job on myself," she hastened to explain.

Dodie followed Hannah out of the garden and up the gently inclined hill toward the house. "So tell me, why would you do chores? I was always glad Dad and Mom decided to work with Uncle Ed in the gravel-contracting business so that I wouldn't have to do farm chores."

Hannah didn't want to delve too deeply into her motives for working on the farm. She didn't know if Dodie would understand or even want to be faced with the stark reality of Hannah's situation.

She knew what she was. A stranger and, to enough Westervelds it seemed, an interloper. She knew many of them didn't think she deserved what she had been given, but they hadn't lived with the consequences of Sam's desertion. She knew that half of the farm was more than she should receive in recompense, but at the same time the part of her that had stayed angry with Sam thought, to some degree, she had earned it.

"I like to keep busy," Hannah said as they walked through the archway of the backyard.

"I see that." Dodie stopped and motioned toward the flower beds. "You've done a lot here. Sam would be pleased."

"It was so overgrown I couldn't stand to see it like this. I planted some seeds here, too. I just wonder when they'll come up."

"They won't flower until late July, maybe early August," Dodie said, bending over to tug an errant weed from the dirt. "But it looks way better than the last time I came to visit…." Dodie's voice drifted away. Of course, being here would remind Dodie of her loss.

"Wow, look at this place," Dodie said as she entered the kitchen. "I haven't seen the house this neat since Grandma Westerveld was alive. You've performed wonders here, girl."

Her compliment eased away Hannah's discomfort, but Hannah still felt self-conscious as she set out glasses, Sam's most likely, and pulled a pitcher from the fridge. Also Sam's. The juice, however, she had bought herself, and the cookies she hastily stacked on a plate.

"Thanks, this is nice," Dodie said, dropping into a chair. She looked around the house again. "I've always loved this place," she said with a wistful sigh.

"Did your grandparents build the house?"

"Yeah. Sam helped. When it was done they had a party. I remember Sam giving out helium balloons, right here in this kitchen. Sometimes I think Sam was just a big kid himself. Grandpa used to wonder if he would take over the farm and then Sam left…"

Hannah finished the sentence for her. "And ended up with my mother."

"Actually I was going to say Sam left to see the world. He got as far as Toronto. Sam was always more of a daydreamer than planner."

"He loved looking at maps," Hannah said, allowing herself to share another memory with this woman. "I remember him showing me all the places he wanted to see yet. I used to worry that he would leave without me.…" She let the sentence trail off as reality intruded on the memory.

"How long did Sam live with you?" Dodie took a bite of her cookie, looking out the dining room window overlooking the lake.

"He started dating my mom when I was three and he moved in when I was six."

Dodie licked the crumbs off her lips and nodded, digesting this information. "What happened to you and your mother after Sam left?"

"We moved. Mom couldn't afford the apartment we had shared with Sam. Our life went pretty much downhill from there."

"Losing Sam must have been hard in other ways, as well."

"He was the only father I knew."

Dodie gave Hannah a melancholy smile. "You sound angry."

Dodie's direct comment eased open the lid Hannah had kept on the questions that had rocketed through her life those many years Sam had been gone. "I keep wondering why he didn't contact us. Never in the thirteen years he was gone did we hear anything from him."

"Nothing?"

Hannah simply shook her head.

"That's odd. My mom said that Sam used to send your mother money pretty regularly."

Bleeding. Tilly's accusing words slithered back into her mind. As she'd promised herself, she had gone looking, but all she had found were some boxes with old clothes and some books.

"No way." Hannah sliced that comment away with a firm hand. "We lived hand to mouth after Sam left. My mom was on social assistance half of the time because she couldn't work. She was sick a lot. We certainly didn't get any money from Sam." Hannah stopped the onslaught of memories and bitterness. It was this house, she reasoned. When Sam left she had imagined him in some amorphous place. Now she was living on his farm, working in his gardens, sitting at the same table he used to sit at. Against her will she began to miss Sam again.

Dodie leaned over and squeezed Hannah's arm.

"Sam wasn't perfect, but he cared about you. Talked about you. We were glad to have him back and were doubly glad when he started going to church again. He said he hadn't gone much when he lived with you and your mother."

"He did at first. Before he moved in," Hannah added, feeling as if she had to defend him.

"Sam had a simple faith and I know that he missed you and was worried about your own spiritual upbringing. I wouldn't be surprised if that's why he put those conditions on the will. So you could experience a Christian community. I know we always wondered what happened to you when Sam came back home. Especially because he said he wasn't allowed to get hold of you."

"What do you mean, wasn't allowed?"

Dodie shrugged. "He told my parents that your mom wouldn't let him talk to you once he left. They thought your mom was punishing him or something like that."

"That can't be." This was not what her mother had told her. This was not what she had grown up with.

That family doesn't care about us. They're ashamed of us.

Those were the words that had resonated through her life.

We've got to take care of ourselves, Hannah. Those Westervelds don't want us. Her mother's voice whispered in her mind, drawing her back to the past and for a moment Hannah felt the piercing sting of disloyalty. Her mother had suffered a lot after Sam left and her mother wasn't here to defend herself.

"No matter what you may have heard, I'm here now and I guess we'll see whether I can stick out the six months Sam stipulated in his will."

"I think you'll do it, though you must get a bit lonely," Dodie said, treating the whole controversial subject of Hannah's legacy with a casual attitude that still surprised her.

"Sometimes." She would like to be able to say she missed Lizzie, but in reality she hadn't given Lizzie and Lizzie's betrayal more than a passing thought in the past few days. Which surprised her considering how angry the situation had made her.

"The church is having a barbecue on Sunday, in a week and a half. You want to come?"

Hannah was taken aback at the invitation. "But I'm not a member."

"That's why I'm asking you. The barbecue is bait to get you to join. Our church is shameless when it comes to bringing in the lost sheep."

Hannah smiled at Dodie's slightly irreverent take on the situation.

"Besides, if you ask Ethan to bring you, it might get his mind on something else besides the farm. During spring planting and fall harvesting it's like he's married to this place."

Hannah thought of the list of messages from various women. "Does he like it that much?"

"This farm is his life. From when he was just a little kid he always said that he and Grandpa and Uncle Sam were going to be farmers together. When Sam was gone, Ethan would skip school to help Grandpa put the crop in."

When Sam was gone, meaning living with her and her mother in Toronto.

"So how did Ethan end up becoming partners with Sam?"

"In high school Ethan worked road construction for my uncle Fred and my dad, but as soon as he graduated, he worked the rigs. Did that for about seven years, putting in long, ridiculous hours and pouring every cent into this place. I remember bugging him because we knew he made good money but he drove the most battered and beaten pickup truck with no muffler. I used to be embarrassed when he would come to church or our family get-togethers."

"Where would you have those get-togethers?" Hannah couldn't seem to stop the questions. The little bit Dodie had told her made her curious about this family and how it worked. And, she had to confess, curious about Ethan, as well.

"Here, mostly." Dodie's attention meandered outside and she smiled. "I remember one time we managed to rope Ethan into playing this silly game. He was supposed to be 'it' and he was chasing Sarah and Marilee. For some reason he ended up running smack into that archway over there and getting tangled up in Uncle Sam's prized trailing roses." Dodie pointed to the wooden structure just outside the window. "Sam was so easygoing, he just sighed, walked out there and tried to hang them up again. They never did grow back well." Dodie laughed again, her eyes looking off into the middle distance.

The ringing of the phone broke into Dodie's reminiscences and, with a flash of annoyance at the interruption, Hannah excused herself to answer it. She glanced at the call display, then picked up the phone.

"Hello, Alana. Ethan isn't in. Do you want to leave a message?" As she spoke she got a pen out of the drawer and started scribbling a note on the message pad. "Yes. I'll tell him." She hung up, pulled the message off the pad and stuck it on the bulletin board that still held messages from the past few days.

"Sounds like you've got this down to a routine," Dodie teased.

"I can't believe how many girls call here for him. Either he really gets around or women here are desperate."

"Ethan doesn't get around," Dodie said, a faint note of defensiveness creeping into her voice.

"He always said he would never, ever go chasing after a woman."

"I'm sorry. It's just he gets a lot of calls."

"Yeah. I know. A lot of girls find him attractive. I just wish he would settle down."

"You sound disappointed."

"He probably would never tell you…" Dodie paused, pushing the cookie crumbs on her plate into a little pile.

Hannah kept quiet, knowing by now that Dodie would fill the silence.

"You know those ditched-at-the-altar stories?" she continued, proving Hannah's assumption correct. "The ones that always sound so farfetched and kind of funny? Well, I never realized how devastating the reality was until I saw it for myself." Dodie was quiet a moment and Hannah's heart grew still. "The day was the rehearsal for Ethan's wedding about three years ago," Dodie continued. "This was the day before the wedding and he was nervous as all get-out. We were, too. None of us were crazy about Colby, no surprise there. I didn't think any girl would be good enough for Ethan. We could never picture Colby living on the farm—she always talked about moving away from here to the city. Always talked about Riverbend like it was a hick town even though she was born and raised here. But here they were, getting ready to get married. Ethan was pacing around the church, making bad jokes, constantly looking to the back of the church for Colby. It was almost as if he knew what was going to happen. Then her dad shows up without her, pulls Ethan aside and tells him Colby changed her mind. He just nodded, as if someone had told him something inconsequential, then started handing out the flowers that were already in the church and taking down the fancy pew markers. We found out later that she called it off because she realized she couldn't live on the farm with Ethan. Thank goodness she left town right after that. We haven't seen her since and her parents don't say much."

Hannah felt her own heart sink at the picture Dodie had drawn for her, imagining Ethan waiting, anticipating. When she had found out that Alex had been fooling around on her, she had felt humiliated, but at least she'd been the one to break things up. She'd had some control.

To have this done so publicly… No wonder he was having trouble settling down. He came across as so self-confident, so, well, cocky, she couldn't imagine that he had been dealt such a humiliating blow.

"I never knew," she said quietly, a sliver of pity pushing its way past the defenses she had built up against his good looks, his appeal.

Dodie reached across the table and grabbed Hannah's arm. "Don't you dare tell him I told you. He'll never buy me another birthday present if he finds out."

Again that light touch of jealousy at the easy connection Dodie had with her family.

"Anyway, I think it's great that you're willing to help out," Dodie continued. "This time of the year Ethan usually gets frazzled and cranky but he seems pretty calm. Maybe now he'll have time to make himself something decent to eat." Dodie shook her head. "He always loses weight during spring seeding and harvest."

"Why is that?"

"Lousy diet. I think the guy lives on cheese and crackers with the occasional wiener thrown in for variety."

"That's disgusting."

"That's Ethan." Dodie checked the time and her eyes grew wide. "Gracious, I've been yapping your ear off too long. I gotta get going." She rose and was about to gather up the plates when Hannah stopped her.

"Please just leave it. You've worked hard enough today."

Dodie waved away her objection. "I love working in the garden. I needed to get out and I really wanted to see you. So I figured gardening was a fairly nonthreatening way to accomplish that."

A peculiar warmth curled around Hannah's heart. "Why did you want to see me?"

Dodie gave her a gentle smile. "Like I said, Hannah, we always wondered what happened to you. Especially because Sam wasn't allowed to know."

Dodie's comment piqued her curiosity. She wanted to ask Dodie more, but she had spent enough time here and, Hannah guessed, probably divulged enough family secrets. She didn't suppose Ethan would appreciate what had transpired at this table, but he wouldn't find out from her.

Dodie stretched again. "You think about that church barbecue, too. You don't need to RSVP, just show up."

"I'll think about it," Hannah said, standing, as well. "And thanks so much for helping me with the seeds and tomato plants. I wouldn't have known what to do."

"Ethan would have been no help. He used to get frustrated with Sam when Sam took time off from seeding to put in his flowers," Dodie said as she walked toward the porch. "You've got enough moisture for now, but if it doesn't rain, you might want to put the sprinkler on it. I'll ask Ethan to rig it up when I get the eggs from his place."

As Hannah closed the door behind her guest, she leaned against it, smiling. Her first visitor had given Hannah a lot to think about.

Ethan. The garden. A broken engagement.

Her mother and Sam.

Dodie's comments sobered Hannah. She must have heard wrong. Marla would never have kept Sam away from her. Hannah knew her mother cried every night after Sam left. She had missed him horribly.

Hannah shook her head as if dislodging the notion. Sam had just given her half his farm. That should be evidence enough for her that he either felt guilty about leaving her and her mother, or he felt Hannah deserved to be here.

And that should be good enough for her.

Chapter Ten

Ethan tapped his thumbs on the steering wheel in time to the music streaming from the tinny radio. The tractor went over a bump, and the radio cut out. He hit the roof of the tractor with his hand and it kicked in again.

"Break down on me one more time, and I'll be back at the dealer trading you in on a brand-new John Deere 9520." Which was an empty and idle threat. He could never afford one of those, but he could dream, couldn't he?

And in his current situation, a dream was all it would be.

Don't think about Hannah, he reminded himself. Don't go there.

But it seemed no matter what happened, he thought about Hannah. Thinking about how her decision was going to affect him, thinking about what he was going to do when she sold her half of the farm. Wondering if she would stick it out. And if she did, how he was going to manage.

Well, the one good thing that had come out of all of this was that he spent more time praying lately. Praying for wisdom, patience, and praying that Hannah wouldn't want to stay.

Though it looked as if she was settling into farm life quite nicely. Putting in a garden, planting flowers, gathering eggs. Feeding the cows.

At first he thought that was just a novelty, but this morning when he was done milking the cow and getting into this tractor to head out to the field, she was already feeding the third bale of hay to the cows. For now, her help was welcome. This was the first spring in many years that he'd been free from at least some of the work. For the past three years, because of the cancer eating away at his body, Sam had been unable to do even the most undemanding of chores.

This was also the first year he had made all the decisions on his own, as well, which was okay, too. Sam was a great partner, but he had some old-fashioned ideas that created unnecessary busywork.

He felt a faint touch of disloyalty but dismissed it. He'd done things Sam's way for many, many years. Now it was time to move on and do things his way.

He came to the end of the field, turned the tractor around, glancing backward as he did to make sure he had the seed drill set exactly right. He dropped the drill, looked ahead and blinked.

Through the dust he saw a figure walking across the seeded field toward him, his dog trotting alongside.

Hannah?

What was she doing way out here?

She stopped in the middle of the field, waiting for him. Scout stood beside her, his tail wagging slowly as Ethan approached.

Hannah wore her long hair pulled back in a ponytail and anchored with one of Sam's old hats. She wore snug blue jeans, a T-shirt and an old flannel shirt of Sam's over top of that.

She looked like a farmer, Ethan thought, smiling at the sight. She looked great.

He stopped the tractor beside her, leaned over and opened the door. "What's up?" he yelled over the noise of the engine.

Hannah pushed her cap back and looked up at him, biting her lower lip. She said something, but he couldn't hear her.

"Come on up," he yelled back, pushing the door open farther.

Hannah climbed into the tractor, swiping at the line of dust on her face. Ethan closed the door and muffled the outside noise.

"Is something wrong?" he asked, wondering why she was looking so dispirited.

"I think I wrecked the other tractor," she said.

His heart sank. Not now. He had just gotten this tractor going; he didn't need another breakdown now. "What happened?"

"I was trying to pick up the last bale and I couldn't get the loader to work. It goes up, but won't go down."

"Can you still drive the tractor?"

She gave him a curt nod. "I parked it by the shop, but I kept it running. I wasn't sure if it would start again."

That couldn't happen, but he was impressed that she was at least thinking ahead. "You can shut it off. Did you walk all the way down here?"

"I figured out where you were working, and then followed the sound of the tractor."

"Here, sit down. I'll drive you back to the road." He pushed aside the jacket and lunch bag on the small ledge between the tractor seat and the door. "You must be tired."

"I'm just worried about the tractor. Are you going to go back and check it right away?" She didn't sit down, choosing to stand beside him, clinging to a handle above the door.

"How many bales did you feed?" He started, put the tractor in gear and started up again.

"Four. I was going for the last one."

"Did you close the gate?"

Her wry look answered that question succinctly.

"I'll take that for a yes."

"I didn't do anything different," she said, as if she needed to plead her case with him.

"Don't worry about it." He turned the radio down, checked the drill, adjusted the PTO and straightened the tractor. Her presence was distracting him and he wasn't sure he minded.

"How long will it take you to finish this field?" she asked.

"I'll quit at five." He wouldn't be done then, but that would hopefully give him enough time to troubleshoot and call Derek at the dealership to order any parts he might need.

"So you won't be able to look at the tractor before that?"

"Sounds like the cows have enough for now. It'll have to wait."

They were coming up to the end of the field but now the road would be a long walk back for her.

"If you're willing to ride back, I'll get you back to where you came from," he said to her.

"Sure."

He got the tractor turned around, and headed back. Though his attention was on his work, he couldn't ignore the girl riding beside him. She didn't smell like vanilla today, she smelled like hay and dust with a hint of diesel. Her hair had bits of straw in it and he could see smudges of dirt and oil on her knees.

She looked fantastic.

Ethan mentally pulled himself back. What was he thinking? He liked his girls blond, cute and smelling like shampoo and perfume.

Yet, as his eyes drifted toward her, he remembered other moments with her. Moments when he felt they shared something more than mere attraction.

He corrected the drift of the tractor. Come harvest he was going to remember this little ride when he came to the bare spots.

Hannah touched his arm and once again his gaze jerked sideways. "You can let me off here. Now that I know where I am, I can cut across country," Hannah said.

He came to a stop but before she got out she asked him, "Anything else I should do with that tractor?"

"I'll have a look at it later," he promised. "Don't worry about it. Just shut it off. It'll be fine." He gave her a reassuring smile as she stepped out. She turned and started walking across the cultivated field, making pretty good time with her long legs, Scout easily keeping up with her.

Ethan waited until she was well away from the tractor and went back to work. But for the rest of the day, his mind wasn't on the crippled tractor back on the farm. He was imagining Hannah working alongside him.

* * *

"You don't have to help me," Ethan said as Hannah handed him a wrench.

"Yes, I do. I feel guilty about wrecking the tractor."

When the loader had gotten stuck up in the air and she couldn't get it down, she was convinced she had broken something beyond repair.

She had dreaded telling Ethan and had put it off as long as she could. The walk took a lot longer than she thought and she got all hot and sweaty, but at the same time, she enjoyed the exertion.

More than that, she enjoyed the sheer freedom of walking across a completely open field that she knew she wasn't trespassing on. Coming from the city, where even looking too long at a person's flowers could be construed as intrusion, the concept was novel to her.

Part of this is mine, she had thought with every step she took, her faithful dog at her side. Actually, Ethan's faithful dog. For now, Scout seemed to be willing to divide his time equally between them. He stayed with her when Ethan was working in the field, with Ethan when he was on the yard, and with her at night.

Now he lay in the shade of the tractor, sleeping, his ears flicking whenever a fly or bug landed on them.

Ethan grunted as he emerged from his contorted

angle behind the loader holding a hose. "Well, your nerves can rest easy. This is a simple fix. You just blew a hydraulic hose. I'll have to order a new one."

"Are they expensive?"

Ethan examined the hose. "This one? You're looking in the neighborhood of four to five, minimum."

"Five hundred dollars?" Hannah's mouth fell open. "For that?"

"More like thousand, actually."

"You must be kidding. Five thousand for that silly-looking thing?"

"Actually I am," Ethan said calmly, wiping the end of the hose with a rag he had tucked in his back pocket. "This one is about fifty bucks."

Hannah pressed her hand against her wildly beating heart. "That's not funny, Ethan."

He winked at her. "No, but the look on your face was priceless."

"You crack me up," she shot back, relief making her knees wobbly. "I had already imagined emptying out my bank account just to pay for some dumb hose."

Ethan looked taken aback. "You certainly didn't think you would have had to pay for this, did you?"

"Well, of course. The tractor broke while I was using it."

He grew serious, his expression intent. "Interesting," he said.

"What do you mean by that?"

"Nothing. Just interesting that you'd be willing to cover the cost of the fix."

Hannah was about to ask him more, but she could see he was anxious to get to the house and make his phone call.

A few minutes later Ethan came storming back to the tractor, his face set in harsh lines.

"Well, that went the way things usually go when I'm ordering parts from Derek," he said, tossing the broken hose into the cab of the tractor. Ethan shoved his hand through his hair, unaware of the grease staining his fingers. "Of course he doesn't have the part in stock. Of course he has to order it in."

Hannah felt sorry for him. She didn't know much about farming, but she caught him looking up at the sky, concern clouding his eyes. Caught him counting to himself, a faint look of panic on his face as she guessed he was calculating how much he had to do and how much time he had to do it in. And whether she wanted to admit it or not, she was pretty sure she factored into his equations from time to time.

When Hannah had first envisioned living on the farm, she'd had no idea what she was getting into. Unfortunately in the past few weeks, she not only had a better idea of how the farm worked, she also knew how important it was to Ethan.

"It will work out," she said, trying to console him. "The cows are fed for now. You've got a couple of days. It will all work out."

His expression softened and he slanted her a crooked smile. "You're trying to make me feel better?"

"Trying. Not so sure if I'm succeeding the way you're still frowning." She was going to smile as she made the comment, and then walk away, casual as can be.

But she couldn't look away and found, to her surprise and dismay, she didn't want to look away. Her heart made a funny little jump. Her fingers itched to brush the smudge of grease off his cheek, to let her hand rest on his shoulder.

She caught herself, but Ethan was the first to break the contact.

He pulled a rag out of his pocket, whistled to Scout and the two of them headed for his trailer.

Hannah walked toward the house, feeling more confused than she had since she'd arrived here.

Chapter Eleven

Ethan paced around the house, clutching the phone while he was on hold, wishing he could be clutching Derek's neck instead.

The little weasel had forgotten to order the hose for the tractor yesterday and was now frantically trying to cover his mistake while Ethan was stuck on hold.

He still had five hundred acres to seed and didn't have time to run around trying to pick up parts. Nor could he pull his big tractor off the field to feed the cows, because the loader that would fit on the tractor was still sitting up in the air on the other tractor.

On top of that, when he had checked the cows, he realized that Angel might be calving tonight. Which meant he had to get her in the barn and check her regularly through the night. He was pretty sure, from her size, that she was going to deliver twins and he needed to make sure they were going to be okay.

"Hey, Ethan, I found the part. It's coming in tonight. You can come and pick it up tomorrow."

He didn't have time for that. "Can't you deliver it?"

As Ethan listened to Derek's yakking about being short-staffed and how all the farmers in the area were trying to get crops in while dealing with breakdowns, his mouth watered at the aromas drifting across his nostrils. The sausages and leftover bread that waited for him in the trailer had lost the limited appeal they might have had compared to the smells he was being subjected to.

"Okay. I guess I'll be in tomorrow." Looked like that was the only option open to him.

Ethan clicked the button to end the call and tossed the phone onto the couch. Then, hoping Hannah hadn't witnessed his flagrant disregard for the frightening neatness of the house, he set the phone in its cradle.

Hannah looked up from the stove as he passed through the kitchen. "Sorry to bother you. I'm leaving now." He involuntarily slowed his steps, and tortured himself by taking another long sniff.

Hannah cleared her throat and Ethan stopped, a spark of hope igniting when she looked his way. But she just gave him a quick smile, then opened the fridge door. Disappointed, he stepped into the porch and slipped his boots on.

"Ethan..."

He poked his head around the corner. "Yes?"

"Do you, uh, want to join me for supper? I was experimenting with a recipe and I think I've got more here than I can eat."

"I don't want to intrude...."

Hannah laughed. "Goodness, Ethan, this is your house, too. Besides, I still feel guilty about the tractor breaking down, so I'd like to make it up to you by asking you to supper."

His stomach rumbled again. Anything was better than what he would be eating in his trailer.

"I'll just wash up in the bathroom," he said. He kicked off his boots and went to the bathroom. One look in the mirror and he shook his head. His dusty hair stood up in all directions, a direct result of his frustration with the tractor and Derek. Dirt and grease smudged his face and neck.

He looked exactly like what he was. A farmer. The kind of person Colby couldn't live with.

So be it. A farmer was exactly what he was and he wasn't ashamed of it. He washed up as best as he could, digging into the cupboard for the old towels that he and Sam always used for drying up after washing the field dirt off themselves.

He cast a longing eye at the spacious shower beside the linen closet, thinking of the narrow little cubby he had in the trailer. Once things were back to normal, he would never take this house for granted again.

The thought drew him up short. Normal. And what shape would that take in six months? He swallowed. Not six anymore. Closer to five. Would he be back in this house? Would Hannah be gone?

Tomorrow will worry about itself. Each day has enough trouble of its own.

The quote from the Sermon on the Mount was one the minister had just preached on last Sunday and one Uncle Sam liked to throw out whenever Ethan started fretting. Which, the first few years they were farming, had been often. Lately Ethan thought he had conquered that particular vice and then his dear uncle, who had taught him not to be concerned about the future, had thrown him a curveball putting that very future in jeopardy.

I'm trying to trust here, Lord, he prayed silently as he dried his face and hands and arranged his hair into some semblance of order. *But You've got to help me out. I'll need more grace than I can muster on my own.*

He gave himself another cursory look in the mirror and shrugged. She'll have to take you as you are, he thought.

Right now he could look forward to eating a hot, home-cooked meal sitting at a real table instead of perched on his bed, watching the news and weather on a fifteen-inch television.

Hannah was setting the table when he returned and he felt the brush of nostalgia. Sam hadn't been as neat as Hannah, but he had always insisted on sitting at the table to eat and afterward, he'd always pulled out the Bible and read a piece from it.

Ethan doubted Hannah would be repeating that particular ritual. She had, however, found a table-cloth and some matching dishes, two minor successes in themselves.

She saw him and said, "Sit down, I'll bring the food to the table."

"I can help." He followed her to the stove, but as he came near, she was turning around, holding a pot. She took a quick step to the side and almost fell, but Ethan caught her by the tops of her arms to steady her.

She looked up at him, her cheeks flushed, her eyes bright. Their gazes held and a peculiar emotion gripped him. Something deeper, stronger than the simple appeal he usually felt around an attractive woman.

He didn't want to let her go.

And as he looked into her eyes, he felt the tenuous beginnings of a connection on a level he had never felt with any girl before. Not even with Colby.

It scared him.

"Sorry about that," she said, pulling gently away.

As he dropped his hands he remembered that moment they had shared in the tractor. Maybe accepting her dinner invitation hadn't been such a smart idea.

Since Colby, he had made it a point to keep a safe distance from the girls he knew. He seldom went on dates with any one girl more than once a month, or he kept the relations so casual that they usually got the hint. But to be attracted to a woman living only a few hundred yards away, a woman he saw every day and who wasn't the least bit interested in him…bad idea all the way around.

He yanked the other pan off the stove and steadied his emotions as he followed her to the table.

"Just put it there," she said, pointing to the hot pad on the table.

She sat down, he followed suit, and now they were facing each other across the table. Just like a married couple.

Don't go there. Don't think that. She's a problem and a complication. In many, many ways.

"Do you usually pray before you eat?" Hannah asked as he tried to corral his out-of-control thoughts. "I mean, if you want to, that's okay. Sam used to at first. When he was dating my mom."

Her comment gave Ethan pause.

"I thought he stopped going to church completely," Ethan said. "I know during family get-togethers I saw a lot of head-shaking whenever the talk turned to Sam's spiritual well-being."

"When he was dating my mother, he took the time to teach me a few prayers and even took me to church. He stopped going when he moved in with us. Which was too bad. I liked going. I think he did, too."

He caught a wistful note in her voice and suddenly felt ashamed that he hadn't stopped by more often to see if she wanted to come to church with him. His assumption had been wrong. And sinful.

"Sam always had a simple faith," he said quietly. "I'm sure he had his own reasons for staying away. When he came back here, he started going again, if that's any comfort."

"It is," she said quietly.

They were both quiet a moment, each seemingly lost in their own particular memories of Sam.

"Why don't you pray before the food gets cold," she said finally, looking down at her plate.

He bowed his head, then started praying out loud. And as he prayed, he felt God's presence surround the two of them, creating a still and quiet center that brought a peace he hadn't felt in months. He paused a moment at the end of the prayer, then looked up to see Hannah, her head still bent.

Had she felt the same emotion, the same aware-

ness of God's presence that he had? He wanted
to ask her, wanted to share the moment, but she
was already standing up and lifting the lid of the
casserole. She served him then herself, and they
ate in silence.

"Sounds like the rain will hold off for a bit," she
said after a while. "Will you get the rest of the
acres seeded?"

He took her little diversion and ran with it. "I
should unless the rain comes sooner."

"I have to confess I'm hoping we get some
soon. I'm a little tired of watering the garden."

Ethan snapped his fingers then. "Sorry. Dodie
reminded me to pick up the sprinkler for you. It's
still at Uncle Dan's."

"Speaking of Dodie, I gave her a call. Told her
that we have some more eggs for her." Hannah
sent Ethan a questioning look. "Does she make
much selling those eggs?"

"No. Even though I give her what I have for free."

"How does she make a living?"

"She has a small consignment store and she
takes some of the more unusual stuff she finds to
the farmer's market. She says she's having fun,
but I don't know. I just wish she'd move out of her
parents' house. Figure out what she wants to do."

He caught Hannah's smile and laughed. "I
know, I sound like a father, but I care about her."

"She's lucky, then."

He glanced at the clock.

"Are you in a hurry?" she asked.

"Sorry. I've got a calving tonight."

"Do you need a hand?"

Ethan gave her a puzzled look. "Why are you so intent on helping?"

"If I'm going to have half this farm, I don't want to sit back and expect it to just come to me."

"The only thing you need to do is stick this out until the end of October and it will."

Hannah looked directly at him. "I expect to try to pay my way when I can. I'm not a freeloader."

"I'm guessing you overheard me talking to the cats. That day you first gathered the eggs."

She didn't say anything, but the faint flush creeping up her neck was evidence enough.

He put down his fork, crossed his arms and leaned forward, determined to make this right. "I'm sorry about that comment. It wasn't fair and it wasn't right. I was frustrated and angry and, I guess, still working through Sam's death."

Hannah pushed the noodles of her casserole around her plate as if sorting through what he was saying. "I heard your aunt say something, too. The day I was in the greenhouse getting plants. She said something about my mom bleeding the farm." Hannah looked up at that. "Where does your family get the idea that we were like that? If we were freeloaders and if my mom did bleed the farm, though I have no idea how in the world that could have happened, why did Sam give me half this farm?"

Why indeed?

But Ethan heard the hurt tone in her voice, remembered Dodie's little chat with him after she'd been here that morning helping Hannah put in the garden. Dodie had reminded him to be careful with Hannah. To recognize that she was weathering her own pain and hurts.

And that she was probably a very lonely person, stuck out here on the farm with no friends and family.

Ethan knew, in his heart, that Dodie was right though he didn't know what he could or should do about it. But now, sitting across from her and hearing the pain in her voice, he felt it personally.

"Sam talked about you while he was back here," Ethan said. "I know he missed you."

"But he never called. Never." Her voice wavered and she lowered her fork.

An awkward silence followed her confession and Ethan didn't know how to fill it. He wasn't sure why Sam had done what he had so he couldn't enlighten her.

"Now I'm sorry," she said, flashing him a self-conscious smile. "I know guys hate the whole tears thing."

Ethan waved away her comment. "When things

get messy, I put my running shoes on." He was used to tears. Colby could turn them on and off at will, especially when she had tried to talk him into moving off the farm. At first he had consoled her, then he had tried to convince her that he loved her *and* the farm.

"Don't worry," Hannah assured him. "I'm not about to go Niagara on you."

He laughed and the awkwardness slipped away.

"You know, I never did find out, exactly how many acres do you own?" she asked.

Relieved to have been spared the potential minefield of women's tears, Ethan plunged into his favorite topic. "I farm about six hundred acres but that's spread out over about six quarter sections of land that I own." Or rather *we* own, he thought. "The rest of that land is pasture and crop land."

The talk moved from land to farming in general. Ethan could have gone on for hours, but he knew from his experience that women's eyes usually glazed over when he went on too long about yields and crop management.

He didn't want Hannah's eyes to glaze over. He wanted them looking at him with that elusive sparkle.

They were finished with the meal all too quickly and Ethan offered to wash up, but Hannah said no.

"You'd better check on that cow."

"I will." Ethan leaned back against the counter,

watching as she put food away, putting the leftovers from the casserole in a plastic container and setting it aside. He should go, but they'd spent a pleasant evening together and he was loath to have it end.

Hannah caught him watching her. "Am I doing something wrong?" she asked.

"Nope. I just miss being here." Too late he realized what that sounded like and how awkward that could make her feel, but to his surprise she nodded.

"I can see that. It's a great little house. I love how the dining room window overlooks the backyard and the lake."

"I think Grandpa and Grandma spent half a year planning this house and where it was going to sit."

"Dodie said that Sam helped build it."

"Yeah. We had a party—"

"With balloons and everything," Hannah put in. "Dodie told me. I have to confess I was a little jealous. I love balloons. Sam bought me one once. Even after all the air had gone out, I kept it tied to my bed."

And again she gave Ethan the tiniest peek into her life with Sam.

Ethan knew he was lingering longer than was polite so he made a show of looking at his watch and pushing himself away from the counter. "Better go check on that cow," he said.

"Will she calve tonight?"

"She'd better. I don't have time to babysit her."
Ethan caught her look and took a chance. "If
you're interested, you can come out and watch."

"You don't mind?"

Ethan shook his head, his eyes on hers. He
didn't mind. Not one little bit.

Chapter Twelve

Hannah stood on the porch looking out over the yard. In the west, the sun pulled the dark behind itself like a blanket over the day. Frogs chortled from the lake beyond the house. Overhead she heard the echoing honk of geese making their way back to their nests.

Contentment.

That's what she felt, Hannah realized. She pulled her light sweater closer around herself, as if to capture the feeling and hold it close. She hadn't felt content for a long time. Her life in the city for the past year had been a matter of getting through each day and hoping the plans she and Lizzie were making would get somewhere.

Living in a cramped apartment above a couple who fought all the time and beside a man who insisted on watching sports channels 24/7 and at full volume had not given her many glimpses of peace.

Or contentment.

Hannah took a long, slow breath in, savoring the tang of the grass, which she had cut this afternoon, that still lingered in the air, the fresh scent of water wafting off the lake.

The silence. It pressed on her ears and surrounded her and she liked it.

And what are you going to do when you go back to the city?

She stopped that train of thought before it could gain momentum. She didn't need to go there at all. Today she was here. Today she was enjoying how the evening cooled the heat of the day, unlike Toronto, where heat was a constant companion, day and night.

Across the darkening yard, a golden rectangle of light shone out from the large, hip-roof barn. A shadow passed in front of the window. Ethan.

She hugged herself tighter. They had already shared a meal, sat across a table from each other and talked like ordinary humans. Almost like a married couple, she had thought at one point.

Not that she would know what that was like. After Sam, her mother had had various men in her life, but they always came in the evening and were gone in the morning. Hannah thought her mother couldn't connect with men again after Sam's desertion.

She could identify. After she left Alex, she had

felt as if this was her future. Men slipping in and out of her life.

But Ethan was so different from any man she had ever met or dated, which gave rise to a curious mixture of anticipation and caution. She shook off her thoughts and stepped off the porch, heading toward the barn. She wanted to see the cow calve.

Scout lay just outside the door. He lifted his head when she came nearer but didn't get up to greet her.

As she bent down to pet him, coming from inside the barn she heard the huff of breath being expelled by the cow. She stepped inside and saw, in the yellow glow of the lantern, the cow lying on its side inside a large pen.

"It's okay, girl. You're okay," she heard Ethan's soft voice reassuring the cow.

Hannah felt a vague tremor at the tenderness in his voice. Hannah was about to retreat when Ethan, sensing her presence, got up and stepped around the partition he must have been leaning against.

"So you did decide to come?"

His smile did more than make her feel welcome. His smile made her suddenly understand all those women who called.

Hannah focused her attention on the cow. "Do you have to watch her the whole time?"

"She's my best cow, so I like to babysit her." He motioned to a square bale parked against the wall, a blanket covering part of it. "Here. I've got a place for you to sit." His consideration added one more little hook in her heart.

"Where will you sit?" she asked.

"At your feet," he said with a glint of humor.

"Perfect."

Was she really doing this? Flirting with a man who was potentially nothing but trouble?

And why not? He was good-looking. He didn't seem to mind dating women on a casual basis. She hadn't spent time with a man in a long while. Ethan was the perfect man to practice on. He knew the rules and played by them. Scrupulously.

Besides, she was going to be leaving here—what did she have to lose?

"So what are you supposed to do while you are here?"

"As little as possible," Ethan said, settling down at her feet, as promised. "She had trouble calving last year and I want to keep an eye on her, make sure everything goes okay this time."

Hannah looked down at the top of Ethan's head, now only inches from her knee. His hair was unruly, spiky, but in an attractive way. She fought the urge to reach over and smooth it.

"That was a good supper," Ethan said, his deep voice quiet now. He drew up one leg and looped his arm around it. "Thanks for letting me share it."

"I'm no gourmet cook," Hannah said, "but I'm glad you liked it."

"Gourmet food is overrated. There's usually not enough and it always tastes bizarre."

"And you know because…" Hannah prompted, teasing him again.

"I'm not just a country hick, you know." Ethan angled her a quick glance, his eyes teasing her back. "I served a term on the Beef Producers board. I've done some traveling, schmoozing with members of other boards in the States and Canada. The meetings were usually held at some ultrapriced hotel with a million pillows and small food portions. I always came back hungry."

"And you promptly filled up on cheese, crackers and wieners like you do now."

Ethan frowned. "How do you know?"

Dodie wasn't exaggerating, Hannah thought. "I hear things. Store them away for future reference."

"Dodie." His single word came out on a sigh and he looked away. "Is that why you invited me for supper tonight? Because you felt sorry for me?"

"Yes."

He shook his head, plucking a piece of straw from his pants and rolling it between his fingers. "I'm crushed. I thought it was my sparkling personality and witty repartee."

"Nope. Pity, plain and simple."

"What else did my dear, babbling cousin spill to you while she was airing the Westerveld laundry?"

She didn't think he would appreciate finding

out that she knew about Colby, so she deflected. "She told me about a disastrous run-in you had with Sam's roses."

"Is nothing sacred?" he moaned.

"And she said that you used to get frustrated when Sam took time off from seeding to plant the garden."

"Never could get through to him that the few bucks he saved growing his own vegetables couldn't compare to the money we lost in downtime."

"But you always got the seeding done?"

"I guess." Ethan smiled, as if remembering. "Sam loved his fresh vegetables. Always said that a person can't get healthy eating store-bought vegetables. Said you could taste the misery and sorrow they were grown in."

Hannah laughed at that. "I loved the taste of the tomatoes Sam planted on our balcony."

"That why you planted some here?"

"You bet. I can hardly wait to try them."

"I hope you're a patient person. You'll be waiting a while," Ethan reminded her.

The cow groaned and Ethan's attention turned back to the job at hand. He got up slowly and beckoned to Hannah, who followed Ethan's lead and moved slowly and cautiously. She didn't want to scare the cow.

"Look," Ethan whispered, taking Hannah gently by the arm and pulling her to his side. He pointed to the back end of the cow. Two tiny hooves were poking out. "It will be just a few minutes now."

Expectation prickled down the back of her neck as she watched. Ethan still held her by the arm and she doubted he was even aware of it. She didn't want to draw his attention to the fact, because she found she wasn't minding the connection at all.

"See. Here comes the head." Ethan's own head was so close to hers she could feel his breath feathering her cheek.

She swallowed, every nerve ending suddenly alive and aware of him beside her. "Do you need to help it along?"

"No. Things are looking good. Better to just let nature take its course."

His hand slipped to her shoulder and Hannah drifted closer to him, her attention mixed between the fascination of the event happening right in front of her and Ethan standing beside her so close they were almost touching.

"Okay, here it comes."

The cow groaned once more, her head lifting with the effort, then the entire calf slipped out.

"C'mon," Ethan said. "I need to make sure it can breathe."

He unlatched a gate and again, drew Hannah through, latching it behind her. He let go of her now, and bent over the calf, looking it over. The calf gave a hollow *bwa* then tried to struggle to its feet.

The cow groaned again and Ethan shot Hannah a triumphant look. "She's having twins."

Two little feet appeared again, then the head, and a minute later another baby slipped onto the straw.

"Careful now," Ethan said, getting up and walking over to Hannah's side. "She's a real quiet cow, but you never know what they're like after birth."

Hannah watched but the cow simply lumbered to her feet, turned, and started licking one of the tiny forms lying in the straw. The one the cow was licking struggled, its feet weaving as it tried to get up. The other simply lay there.

She watched, a sense of wonder coursing through her at the sight. Those two tiny beings had been inside of that cow only a few moments ago. Now, here they were, fully formed, alive and trying to get up.

One still lay on the straw, not moving. "Is that one okay?" Hannah asked. "Shouldn't you help it out?"

"He's probably just tired." Ethan sounded so relaxed and calm, but Hannah willed the little calf to get up. Then it lifted its head, gave it a shake as if trying to orient itself to its new surroundings and it, too, tried to struggle to its feet.

"They're so cute," Hannah breathed, kneeling down to get a better angle. "And so small compared to the other ones out there already."

"Twins are always smaller, but Angel's a good milker. They'll catch up in no time."

The cow continued to lick the calves, the rasp of her tongue audible in the quiet of the barn. As Angel licked, from deep within her came the occasional lowing sound.

Hannah knew the word but had never realized how appropriate it was until she heard it emanating from this cow. It sounded peaceful, comforting. Motherly.

"You can see how rough her tongue is," Ethan explained, kneeling down beside Hannah, as well. "When she licks the calves, she helps their circulation get going. Gets them warm."

One calf was finally on its feet, wobbling, its legs trembling.

"I can't believe they can get up so fast." She chanced a sidelong look at him. He was watching the calves, a tender look on his face that made her heart tremble.

"Look. He's trying to drink."

Hannah forced her attention back to the calves and couldn't look away. The one wobbled, fell, got up and then slowly made its way to the back end of the cow, nosing around but missing the mark completely. He gave another throaty bawl and got turned around, facing the cow's front. He bawled again, a plaintive sound that made Hannah want to help.

The cow was busy licking the second calf, unconcerned that its other baby was making a complete hash of trying to get its first meal.

"C'mon, you silly thing," Hannah whispered. "Get turned around. You'll never get a drink that way."

"Frustrating to watch, isn't it?" Ethan said.

"Oh look," Hannah said. "I think the first one is catching on."

The calf, still wobbling on its feet, had finally gotten turned around and was nosing the cow's bag. Then, finally, they could hear the sound of the calf drinking.

"This is amazing," she said softly, enthralled by the sight of the two baby calves, their mother the picture of contentment.

"Isn't it? I've seen this a hundred times and it never, ever gets old." Ethan rested his hand on her back as if celebrating this moment of connection.

He probably acted this way with all the girls who did this with him. He was probably no different from Alex, the cold voice of reason reminded her.

Hannah was tired of the cold voice of reason. She and Ethan had just shared a meal; now they had shared an experience. And she wanted to sit a few moments longer, welcoming the sense of unity his touch created.

She heard his contented sigh. Their faces were close enough that she could see the flecks of green in his eyes, see a faint sprinkling of dust glinting on his long, thick eyelashes.

All she did was smile. Just a simple, cautious smile.

His hand came to her face, touched her cheek. Her own hand came up and anchored his.

Then he leaned closer. She met him halfway and their lips touched each other, gently at first, then again.

Hannah's world tipped and everything she knew changed, altered and rearranged. She didn't want the kiss to end, but knew it had to stop.

Yet when she drew back, she couldn't keep her eyes from his.

"Hannah," he whispered, a whole world of feeling in that one word.

She kept her hand covering his and gently stroked his rough fingers with hers.

You've got to stop. You know what he's like. You're just another in a long line of girls.

This moment, this time—her mind knew it was dangerous, but her heart yearned for this. She could play this game a while, she reasoned. Nothing wrong with that.

But as her eyes held his, as she saw his expression soften and, as his fingers lightly caressed her face, the guarded part of her heart trembled.

She bent closer and brushed her lips across his again, then drew away.

There. She was in charge. She knew what she was doing and for now, what did it matter?

A bawl from the calf and an answering one from the cow pulled her attention back to where they were. That bawl sounded a warning knell in her mind.

The cow was looking right at them, raising and lowering her head as if to say, *Get out of here.*

Thoughts of cow number 55 raced through her head and she scrambled to her feet, glancing over her shoulder for the gate.

Ethan got up, as well, but he was laughing. "You're okay. She's not fussed, just telling us she knows we're here and to keep our distance."

Hannah felt foolish but at the same time thankful for the segue away from intimacy.

And now what? Stay and make casual conversation? Hannah had dated other guys before, but usually the kiss came at the end of the date, in front of the apartment, which created an automatic out.

What was she supposed to do now?

"We should leave them be," Ethan said, resting his hand on her shoulder as he ushered her out of the pen. "Let them bond. Now that I know the calves are okay, I can leave them for the night."

Hannah took a last look at the results of the miracle she'd seen. Both calves were drinking now and she smiled.

And she'd been kissed by Ethan.

She wasn't so sure what to do with that memory.

"Well, I'd better get back to my trailer." Ethan lowered his hand as they left the barn. "Got a busy day tomorrow."

"You have to get that part?"

"Yeah, but I really don't have time." He shook his head as he turned off the light and shut the door.

"Is there another way I can feed the cows?"

"You see how big those bales are. The tractor is the only way. It's not a difficult fix, but running to town will take more time than I have."

Darkness had slipped across the sky while they were in the barn. The frogs had stilled their chorus for now and the only sound was the warbling trill of a bird.

Hannah stopped to listen. "What is that?" she asked.

Ethan stopped, too, and kept his hand resting on her shoulder, maintaining the light connection begun in the barn. "A nighthawk. They make that sound as they're diving." He looked up, then his hand tightened on her shoulder, urging her around. "Look over there," he said. "In the sky."

She did as she was told, then her mouth fell open. Swatches of light, green and blue edged with orange, danced across the sky, waving, undulating, a silent curtain of color and light.

"Are those—"

"The northern lights."

She stared as they waved and shot upward, then faded, only to be replaced by another ethereal band of light.

The sheer wonder and beauty of this phenomenon rendered her speechless.

"They don't often show up in the spring." Ethan's voice was a quiet rumble behind her.

A band of green shot across the sky, then solidified for a heartbeat. Shifting and changing, it moved upward. She lost her balance watching and Ethan steadied her. But he didn't let go.

She shivered both at what she was seeing and at his touch and he misinterpreted the action.

"You don't have a sweater," he said, slipping his arm around her to pull her back against himself. "You must be cold."

She was going to make a comment about his lame line, but then the light intensified and grew and she was speechless once again.

"'When I consider the heavens, the works of thy hands, the moon and the stars which thou hast ordained,'" he said as they watched.

It sounded familiar. "What's that from?"

"The Psalms. My mom used to make us memorize passages of Scripture when we were younger. Can't remember all of them, but I do remember that one."

"How does the rest go?" she asked, a memory teasing her mind.

"'What is man that thou art mindful of him? Or the son of man that thou visitest him? For thou hadst him a little lower than the angels...'"

As Ethan continued, Hannah let the words wash over her, resurrecting the memories.

"That sounds like what Sam used to recite, sitting on the balcony on one of our rickety kitchen chairs, looking up at the sky."

As the memory returned, full-blown, her throat thickened. Why was she so sad about Sam now? He hadn't been in her life for a long while, yet as she allowed the memory to solidify and take root, her sorrow grew larger.

Even as reason battled with memory, she felt as if Ethan's words bridged the distance between then and now, between there and here.

She turned and looked up at him, their gazes locked, and Hannah's breath caught in her throat. He was going to kiss her again.

Instead, his arms came around her and he drew her close, resting his chin on her head. His chest lifted. Hannah slipped her arms around him, relishing the reality of holding and being held by someone larger and stronger.

A light sigh drifted from her lips as she laid her head against his chest. She closed her eyes and rested there. The loneliness that had nipped at the edges of her life with annoying regularity the past couple of years dissipated in Ethan's arms.

Just for a moment, she thought. I'm just letting this happen for a moment, and then I'm going to pull away.

His hand touched her head and his fingers tangled in her hair.

Now. Pull away now, she thought as he gently drew her head back. Don't kiss him again or you're going to be lost.

His fingers caressed her scalp as his eyes held her gaze.

"Hey, Hannah," he said, his voice a rumble in his chest.

His eyes followed the path of his fingers through her hair, coming to rest on her cheek.

As her heart slowed, she swallowed and realized that she had to stop this. Now.

"Hey, Ethan," she said, surprised that her voice sounded so even. Steady. "Thanks for showing me." She stepped back. "I hope you sleep well."

And she was walking away.

Don't look back. Do not look back.

But it wasn't as easy as she thought. She wanted to see his reaction, look at him one more time. But if she was to keep hold of her heart, she had to stay the course. Stay focused on the house and don't look back.

She heard the thump of Scout's feet on the wooden steps of the deck and he was standing beside her, panting, looking up at the door.

She bent down and stroked his head, thankful for the company.

"You supposed to keep watch?" she asked, fluffing his ears. She opened the door and then, as if she couldn't help it anymore, looked back.

But Ethan was gone.

Chapter Thirteen

She couldn't sleep. And no wonder. She hadn't kissed anyone since Alex.

Who did she think she was fooling with her cosmopolitan, "I can take care of myself" act? She wasn't going to be winning any Oscars with that one. Kissing Ethan had been a mistake.

Hannah flopped onto her side wishing she could hit Rewind. If she could do it over again, she would have stayed in the house and away from the sight of Ethan with that cow.

Then she wouldn't be lying here, remembering the feel of his lips on hers one second and trying to kick herself the next.

She glared out the window as if blaming the remnant of the bright colors for her second mistake.

When I consider the heavens. The words Ethan had recited slipped back into her mind. *What is man that thou art mindful of him?* Did God really care about her? Had he seen what had just happened between her and Ethan?

She thought of other pieces of the Bible Sam would recite when he and her mom were only dating. *As a father has compassion on his children...* She remembered that one because Sam would smile at her when he read that.

And what compassion had he had on her? He had given her the farm but, she realized now, she would relinquish all that just for some explanation of why he had left them alone.

"Help me, Lord." The simple prayer was an automatic one for self-preservation. Yet, as she spoke the words aloud, she felt as if she had released some control of her life to God, to Someone who had intimate and eternal knowledge. Not only of her, but of Sam and Ethan, as well.

When Hannah and her mother had gone their separate ways and Hannah had helped her mother clean out the apartment they shared at the time, she had found Sam's Bible. The first year he lived with them he would take it out from time to time and read it to her. But then he put it away. She wondered if his guilt over his living situation kept him from reading the Bible and going to church.

She wasn't sure why she had packed it before coming here. Maybe it was for this time, she thought, flinging on her housecoat. She padded across the floor, Scout right behind her. The Bible was in the same place she had put it when she had unpacked.

She pulled it off the shelf and crawled back into bed, turning on the bedside light. Though her mother didn't approve of Sam reading the Bible to her, Hannah had loved sitting beside him, listening to his deep voice.

As she leafed through the book, she felt it again. The faint sting of betrayal. Staying here, in Sam's house, surrounded by Sam's family, didn't help lessen that feeling, but at least he'd had the grace to try to make it up to her.

Hannah thought of how she had ended up here. Certainly not the life she had planned. But hopefully, with the money she got from this place, she would have a good start on her own plans. She thought of the move back to Toronto, finding another apartment, trying to find work. The money she got from the farm would help finance another business.

Back in Toronto? And Ethan?

Her fingers crept up to her lips, as if remembering Ethan's kiss. She closed her eyes, wishing she could go back and recapture that moment of weakness.

Did she really?

She flipped through the pages of the Bible, distracting herself from the memory insidiously working its way to the forefront of her mind.

She started to read randomly. And as if God was also determined to mock her sense of self-reliance, the words in front of her were the same words Ethan had recited only a few hours ago.

She went back to the beginning of the Psalm and read from there.

"O Lord, our Lord, how majestic is your name in all the earth! You have set your glory above the heavens. From the lips of children and infants you have ordained praise..." Hannah thought of the display of color she had seen. This Psalm had it right. God had indeed set his glory above the heavens. She read on and paused at verse four. "What is man that you are mindful of him and the son of man that you care for him? You made him a little lower than the heavenly beings, and crowned him with glory and honor."

Hannah thought of this vast world, of the small part she had seen out of the window of the airplane, and at the same time her mind turned to the handful of seeds she and Dodie had planted. Since that time, as Dodie had promised, they had been transformed into row upon row of baby plants, each with their own unique leaf pattern and structure. This afternoon she had been on her hands and knees, studying the tender curl of a bean sprout, its leaves still encased in the husk of the seed pod it had sprung from.

She thought of the calves she had seen born. Life and birth. God watching over all, according to this Psalm, caring for not only the earth, but also all the people in it. This earth, which was just a speck in the universe.

Hannah read further. The Psalm said that God had made man ruler of this earth, over "...all flocks and herd and the beasts of the field." Like Ethan with his cows and the fields he planted.

Her heart softened, remembering the look on Ethan's face as he had watched the cow with her calves. She had never seen such a look of tenderness on any man's face before.

Her heart fluttered and to keep her mind from going down that dangerous road, she turned back to the Bible.

She closed the Bible and walked down the stairs and onto the porch. Sleep was further from her than before. Was she being foolish allowing Ethan into parts of her life and heart that she hadn't even shared with Alex?

She sat on a chair, its wooden seat cool as she wrapped her housecoat around her. Scout followed her, dropping onto the deck. Above her the glory of the northern lights no longer competed with the stars that were now ablaze in the sky.

Did God see her now? Did He truly care as the Psalm said He did?

Scout raised his head and emitted a gentle

whine. Hannah followed the direction of his look and saw a figure walking across the yard to the barn. Ethan.

How was she supposed to deal with him? She had five months to go.

Help me stick with my plan, Lord, she prayed, knowing that she needed divine intervention to make it out of Riverbend with her heart intact.

It was early morning. Ethan sat with his head buried in the flank of the milk cow, the hollow echo of the milk squirting onto the bottom of the pail telling her that he had just begun.

The cow and her twins were lying down in their pen beside the milking stanchion. The calves' ears flicked now and then, chasing away flies.

Hannah stayed in the doorway, preferring to keep her distance. Distance was good. Distance was important.

The sharp light of day had brought her in sync with the sharp voice of reason warning her about last night.

She had made a colossal error thinking she could treat any kind of relationship with Ethan casually. She wasn't a casual person. Everything she did, she did with her whole heart.

And her heart was in danger of slipping out of her grasp if she kept up this flirtation with Ethan. If she let him kiss her again.

Scout saw Ethan, wandered over to his side and flopped down in the straw.

"Hey, there, buddy," Ethan said, then half turned and gave Hannah a smile that pulled at her heart.

"Good morning," she said, injecting a note of complete casualness into her voice. Distance. Keep your distance.

"Back atcha. Did you have a good sleep?"

Sam had always asked her the same question, and hearing it from Ethan wore at her resolve to keep up the barriers.

"Like a log."

"Getting used to the country then." He gave her another smile, then returned to his milking. The kittens wandered out to join him, sitting in a row, waiting.

"I got pulled out of bed last night by a phone call from Pearl. She said she wanted you to call her back."

"Sorry about that. I'll tell her not to call you at home anymore."

"Doesn't matter." She needed the reminder of the other women in Ethan's life.

But he turned to her, his expression serious. "To me it matters."

Did she dare let the implications of his words, underlined by his intense regard, settle into her life?

She could almost feel his lips on hers again as

their eyes met. With a mental shake of her head, she focused on her reason for coming here instead.

"When you were talking to Derek, you said that you didn't have time to run in and get the part. Did you want me to?"

"You don't need to be my errand boy. Girl."

Hannah scooped up one of the kittens, cradling it against her face. "I'm the one who broke the tractor, after all."

"How many times do I have to tell you, you didn't break it." He shot her an annoyed glance that turned into a smile when he could see that she was teasing him.

Hannah peeked over the wooden fence separating the cow and her calves from the rest of the barn. "How are mother and children doing?"

"Really good. I just have to give the calves an ear tag, and their shots, and they can all go into the main corral."

"I'm not going to offer to help you with that," she said, shuddering, thinking of the bright yellow tags each of the baby calves sported, printed with the number of their mother so they could be identified.

"No different than getting your ears pierced," he said with a laugh.

"And how would you know how that feels?" she asked, still watching the calves. One got up, slowly stretched its front legs, then its back and trotted over to his mother's side and began drinking noisily.

"I was a rebel at one time in my life," Ethan said.

"You had your ear pierced?" She tried to imagine Ethan, the poster boy for redneck Alberta, with a pierced ear.

"I also played drums in a heinously bad rock band."

"Wow. You were a bad boy."

"Ask my mom."

"I'll go one better. I'll ask Dodie."

"She'll just lie," he said with a grin.

Hannah blew gently on the kitten's face, laughing as the kitten squinched up its eyes. "Where are the keys to your truck? Where is the tractor dealership, and how do I pay for the part?"

"You're not going to give up, are you?"

She shook her head, brushing her chin over the kitten's ears.

"Okay. Keys are in the ashtray of the truck. There's more than enough gas to get you to town. Preston, if you want."

"Edmonton, so I can do a shopping marathon?"

"I can't imagine you charging your way through the mall."

His comment, combined with a smile that he gave her over his shoulder, created a gentle warmth deep within her.

"You can charge the hose to my account," he

continued, turning back to his job. "And if you wait until I'm done here, I'll draw you a map of how to get to the dealership."

A few minutes later, Hannah waited outside Ethan's trailer while he wrote her instructions. The trailer rocked a bit as Ethan moved around, and once again Hannah felt a stab of guilt for being the one to put him out of that charming house. She was the interloper; she should be the one staying in the trailer, not him.

He came outside again, holding a piece of paper. "This is the part you need and here're the directions."

Hannah looked it over. "Where's downtown from here?"

Ethan took the paper and scribbled a map. He gave her another crooked smile, which did nothing for her equilibrium. He let it linger just a moment, his eyes caressing hers. She swallowed, wondering if he was going to kiss her again. But instead, he walked away, whistling.

Hannah swallowed, wishing she could be as casual about the whole thing as Ethan.

But as she drove to town, she pushed aside her concerns, preferring to concentrate on the sun pouring down, the open road ahead of her and the horsepower at her command.

She opened the window to let the fresh spring air flow into the cab of the truck, turned up the stereo and soon was singing along to Paul Brandt, tapping her fingers on the steering wheel.

As the land rolled past her, she drew in a long, slow breath, enjoying the feeling of being on top of the world afforded to her courtesy of a Dodge pickup with a lift kit.

Things were going okay, she thought, her mind flicking back to Ethan's gentle touch. His kiss.

Definitely okay.

And as long as she kept her focus, she should manage Ethan just fine.

Hannah put the glasses on the tray and, on the saucer, carefully arranged the cookies she had just baked. The leftovers from her dinner were parceled out—two packages for Ethan and one for her.

He was supposed to come for dinner tonight, but she had waited too long to ask him. He had other commitments, he'd said with enough disappointment to allay her own.

It had been a week since he had kissed her beneath the northern lights. A week since she had waited for him to find another opportunity.

But he'd kept his distance.

When Sunday came, she found she wanted to go to church but was unsure how to approach him. So she stayed behind and read a piece from the Bible instead.

Then, Monday evening, he had stopped by on

his way to his trailer to tell her that he was celebrating. He was done seeding. She was sitting on the porch, eating a cookie made from a recipe Dodie had given her. He asked for one and a few minutes later was sitting beside her, drinking iced tea and talking about his day.

Their quiet conversation eased away a modicum of the tension that had sprung up between them, and when he stopped by Tuesday night, she was ready with an extra cup of tea and more cookies on the plate.

That was when she had asked him to come to supper tonight. And that was when he told her, with a disappointed smile, that he had a meeting to attend. But was it okay if he stopped by later?

And now she was watching the clock, wondering what time he would come by. What would they talk about tonight?

Would he try to kiss her?

Her hands stilled as her mind slipped back to their last kiss. In the past few weeks, for the first time in her life, she felt her life approaching a level of peace she hadn't experienced before.

She knew she was falling for Ethan and though she didn't dare presume on his feelings, she did dare to think he felt something for her. She hadn't imagined the connection that sparked between them when their eyes met, whenever his hand brushed hers.

The ring of the phone pierced Hannah's errant thoughts, and she jumped.

"Hi, is Ethan there?" The breathless voice made Hannah sigh.

"He's not, but I can take a message."

"Who are you?"

She must be new, Hannah thought, pulling out the message pad. Most of the other girls had either stopped calling or they assumed she was no threat and baldly asked her to make sure Ethan called them. Immediately.

Which he never did.

"I'm Hannah," she said, forgetting to give her usual response.

"Hannah who?"

"Who is this?" she parried, suddenly unwilling to explain her tenuous relationship with Ethan.

"Okay. I'll play. This is Colby. I know he's not married, so you must be a girlfriend. Tell him I really need to talk to him. Now, if possible."

A sliver of panic shot through Hannah. The almost-wife. The one that Ethan didn't want to talk about. "I'm sorry. All I can do is pass on the message."

"I'm guessing from the defensive tone of your voice that you're the latest girlfriend. That poor guy. He must be so lonely." A plaintive note entered her voice. "I was so stupid to break up with him," Colby whispered, sounding utterly distraught. "And now I'm in such trouble. I need his help. Tell him I really need to see him."

Hannah couldn't stifle the flash of annoyance she felt at Colby's insistent tone, but she kept her voice even. "I'll tell him that you called. Does he have your number?"

"He probably knows it by heart." This was followed by another sniff and then a click.

Hannah found a pencil and a piece of paper as her thoughts swarmed like bees, filling her head with noise.

Colby. The girl that Ethan had been going to marry. She needed to talk to him. Urgent.

Hannah wrote out the note, surprised to see her hands trembling. What did Colby want with Ethan and what would his reaction be?

She studied the plate of cookies, the teapot waiting for the hot water. Maybe she should cancel this little assignation and go straight to bed. She was walking a tenuous line and might already have veered too deeply into dangerous territory. No sense encouraging something doomed to end.

And it was, she reminded herself as she walked to the kitchen. She was leaving and when she did, she wouldn't have Ethan's blessing. She'd have half his farm.

She reached for the light switch, then jumped as a face showed itself in the window.

Ethan. He was smiling at her and miming drinking a cup of tea.

Hannah's hand hovered over the light switch, but then whimsy crowded out reality and she smiled back.

Five minutes later she sat beside Ethan, pouring tea, acting as if the phone call she had just received hadn't created a seismic shift in her life.

Ethan smiled through the steam drifting upward from the teapot. Would that smile change when she told him about Colby? She knew she had to pass the message on, but was reluctant to bring up her name. Colby hadn't been a mere distraction. She'd once been Ethan's fiancée. To bring her into the conversation now would change everything. And Hannah wanted Ethan's attention for as long as possible.

She set down the pot and some tea slopped out of the spout.

"Not the cookies," Ethan cried out, rescuing the plate from the overflow. "These look like your best effort yet."

The small praise brought forth a bloom of warmth. "These were the easiest to make so I hope they taste good."

Ethan took a bite, released a sigh and leaned his chair back on two legs. "Does it get much better than this? Tea on the porch after a day's work, eating homemade cookies." His glance grazed over her as if adding her presence to the list of his favorite things. Then he leaned over and gently wiped a finger over the corner of her mouth. "Chocolate smear," he said.

His casual touch robbed her of speech, but Ethan seemed more than content to sit back, eat cookies and let the warbling of the frogs and the faint howl of coyotes fill the silence.

Scout raised his head and growled lightly, a gentle warning to the coyotes.

"Easy, Scout. They're just playing around." Ethan patted the dog lightly on the head and Scout sighed, dropped his head on his paws and let his eyes drift shut again.

Ethan tilted his chair back as he took another sip of tea. His one hand hung from the armrest of the chair, while he steadied the mug with his other hand. He looked completely at ease, Hannah thought with a small measure of frustration. She would have enjoyed the casual give and take of the conversation more if Colby's name wasn't thrumming through her head.

"How are things coming along on the tractor?" she said, determined to keep trying.

"Nice to have that done before Sunday." He massaged the back of his neck.

"That's the day of the barbecue, isn't it?"

He nodded.

"And that's after the church service?"

He turned to her, his expression serious. "You don't need to go to church to go to the barbecue."

"No. I knew that. I just thought…" She let the sentence drift off, unsure of how to articulate her thoughts. "I'd like to go to the service. I would have liked to go before."

Ethan held her gaze, then, in spite of the gathering dark, she saw a faint flush stain his cheeks. "I should have asked you last Sunday. I'm sorry. I shouldn't have assumed… I'm sorry."

She waved away his objections. "I could have asked."

"So, why do you want to go?"

Why indeed? She hesitated, searching for the right words. "I've been reading the Bible lately. Trying to pray." She shrugged, suddenly self-conscious. "But I don't know where to start or how."

"I think God understands," Ethan said quietly. "I'm glad you're coming."

Her cheeks warmed. "I'm not a complete neophyte. I went to church with Sam when he was dating my mother," she said, allowing the memories to creep back. "Now that I'm here, where Sam used to live, I just feel it's important I go again."

"Did your mom ever go with you and Sam?"

"When Sam moved in with us, he stopped going. Mom wasn't much for church. Said it was for weaklings."

"She was right."

Hannah shot him a puzzled look. "What do you mean?"

"It's like that passage in Corinthians, where Jesus says to Paul, '"My power is made perfect through weakness."' I like to know God can use me when I'm not that strong. Especially when I'm not that strong."

Ethan spoke with a conviction intrinsic to his character. He knew what he wanted, he knew what he believed. He lived his life on a solid foundation with his eyes facing forward.

She wished she had one iota of his certainty. Her entire life had been one of adjusting on the fly, making plans and discarding them as circumstances forced decisions.

But now she felt she was settling in here. Making a place and making plans that had a future.

A shiver trembled down her spine. Plans for what? In less than five months she would be leaving, taking her so-called inheritance with her.

Wouldn't she?

"So how's the rest of the garden?" Ethan's innocent question scattered the questions that tangled her thoughts and brought them once again to safe, easy ground.

"I thinned the carrots today," she said, taking refuge in the mundane and ordinary. "Some of the flowers in the back garden are up."

"Should have a good bunch of tomatoes, too, from the way those plants are growing. I hope that rain they keep forecasting comes. If we get the moisture we need we'll have a good crop."

We'll have a good crop. He was including her in the future.

And Colby's name slithered into her mind once again. She couldn't put it off any longer. His ex-fiancée hung like an unwelcome specter and needed to be dealt with.

"By the way, Colby called. Left a message. Said it was urgent." She threw the words out casually, as if they didn't create a tempest of uncertainty in her own heart.

"When?"

"Just an hour or so ago."

"Why is she calling me now? After all this time? I haven't heard anything from her for a couple of years and now..."

Hannah felt a nudge of disappointment at his questions. She had half hoped he would simply say, yeah, whatever, as he did whenever she passed on messages from any other woman.

"Colby said that it was really important that she talk to you," Hannah said, hoping to shed a bit of light on his questions.

Ethan took another sip of his tea, again rocking his chair back on two legs. But he wasn't smiling anymore. They sat in silence, the faint howling of coyotes laying a counterpoint to the breeze rustling the leaves.

Ethan dropped his chair down, put his mug on the tray and stood.

"Church starts at ten if you're still interested."

She didn't look up, startled and dismayed by his abrupt shift in topic. Then, to her surprise, he placed his hands on either side of her chair, bent over and dropped a light kiss on the top of her head.

"Good night, Hannah," he whispered. Then walked away, leaving her in a stew of uncertainty and confusion.

Chapter Fourteen

She slipped into bed and stared up at the ceiling, her mind spinning. She had told Ethan about Colby and then he had kissed her.

She didn't understand what was going on. Didn't understand where to file away what information.

Colby. Ethan. The woman he'd nearly married.

Why did she care so much about this woman who at one time had held Ethan's heart? Why was this girl jumping back into Ethan's life? Why didn't she leave him alone?

She rolled over onto her side, yanking the sheets around herself.

Scout whined a little, as if to tell her to settle down, but after half an hour of thoughts and worries chasing each other, she gave up. She needed to find something to occupy her mind.

She remembered the cupboard where she'd put

a lot of Sam's personal things. Maybe there'd be a book in there to keep her busy mind occupied.

She stepped into Sam's room, snapped on the light and walked over to the cupboard. Inside she found the pile of books she'd been looking for, but she knew there was a box that had a better selection.

She knelt down and pulled the first box out and looked inside. The box only held old clothes.

When she'd first overheard Tilly's comments about Sam sending her mother money, Hannah had gone looking through the house for evidence to prove the woman wrong. All she had found was these few boxes holding an odd assortment of books and clothes that she had set aside for Ethan to discard.

But instead of throwing them away, he'd walked back upstairs with them and put them back in Sam's room. She hadn't touched them until now.

She picked out a shirt and held it up, wondering if it was Sam's. She gave it a quick sniff, wondering if anything of his remained. The faintest whiff of cologne teased her nose, but mostly the shirt smelled musty—like old paper. She riffled through the shirts, looking for some more books. Halfway down, she found a stack of envelopes bound with an elastic band. Curious, she pulled out the rest of the shirts and uncovered more envelopes.

She pulled one package out and her heart stilled.

Bank statements. The ones she'd gone looking for.

If Sam had sent her mother money, as people assumed, surely she would find the evidence here?

Hannah pulled the box out of the cupboard and as she opened it, a surprising sense of foreboding hovered over her.

Bleeding. Freeloading.

No. Neither described the mother she knew. Hannah deliberately resurrected humiliating memories of going to the food bank, of trying to find innovative ways to put together clothes that she bought at thrift shops, hoping, praying that she wasn't showing up in a fellow classmate's castoffs.

She yanked back the flaps and started with the bank statements and canceled cheques. Looked as if Sam had kept everything, she thought, sneezing as age-old dust was resurrected by her burrowing. Some were organized in envelopes with the date neatly written on the outside, some were randomly dropped in the box.

Half an hour later she had them sorted and lying out on the floor. They only went back twelve years, but that might be sufficient. She picked up the oldest ones and flipped through January's canceled cheques. Nothing made out to Marla Kristoferson. Ditto for February, March, April...

She made short work of the other years, feeling as if she had single-handedly restored her own faith in her mother. With a sense of relief she wrapped the cheques in the statements again, snapped the rubber bands around them and put them back in their envelopes. The Westervelds were wrong about her mother and about her.

She regarded the box of letters she had put to one side. She didn't want to delve into Sam's personal life, but curiosity won out over discretion and she quickly flicked through those letters, as well, then stopped when she saw one addressed to Sam.

From her mother.

Hannah's heart pushed up into her throat as, with trembling fingers she pulled the envelope out of the box.

Was this letter a plea for him to come back? Had it touched him in any way? She checked the faded postmark. Eight years ago.

For a moment Hannah simply held the letter in her hand, brushing a fingertip over her mother's writing. Her heart hitched as sorrow tugged at her emotions. She fought back. She couldn't allow her grief to pull her down.

Hannah removed the letter from the envelope and unfolded it slowly, reading the precious words her mother had scribbled out almost eight years ago.

"…you have to stop asking if you can see Hannah. She's not your daughter and you have no right. BTW we're moving again, but I'll be keeping the same bank account 'cause this time, we're going to stay in the same city. So send the money to the place you always did. The money is a real help for Hannah and me. I hope she decides to go to college. Would you spring for that? Better go. Marla."

What was this?

Hannah read the letter again, then as the words registered, icy fingers gripped her temples and a chill feathered down her spine. The letter fell out of her cold fingers, her mother's own words destroying the world Hannah had painstakingly built.

Sam is gone. He doesn't want to be a part of your life.

These were the words Marla had thrown at her each time she caught Hannah crying over the loss of Sam.

But her mother had lied to her. Sam had asked if he could see her and Marla had refused him the right. Hannah read the letter again, then as her heart skittered in her chest, she dug through the box, but her search unearthed only one more letter, dated seven months ago. When Marla was diagnosed with stomach cancer.

Hannah set the letter aside. She didn't want to read it yet. She still had to wrap her mind around what she had just discovered.

How could her mother have gotten the money when Sam had never written her any cheques?

Hannah dug back into the box and randomly

selected a bank statement. Two years old. She opened it and this time she laid out a couple of statements side by side. The one thing they all had in common was an electronic transfer every month from Sam's account to the same place. As if to prove this unequivocally, Hannah pulled out the last five years' worth of statements, laid them out in order and combed through them all.

But nothing changed. Each month Sam had sent money to a bank account and as the years passed the amount increased.

It wasn't a huge amount, but it would have been enough to keep Hannah and Marla going, which, apparently, it had. All these years Hannah had been embarrassed because she thought her mother was collecting welfare, when she was doing exactly what the Westervelds had accused her of.

Bleeding. Freeloading.

Hannah pressed her face to her hands. *I didn't know,* she wanted to shout out. *My mother never told me.*

And as she silently protested her innocence to the darkened room, another reality slithered into place.

The family had been right. Ethan had been right. She didn't deserve to be here. Sam had more than paid for leaving her and her mother. He didn't have to leave her half his farm.

And Ethan, who had put so much into the farm, was right in thinking she didn't deserve any of this.

Ethan who had kissed her.

She closed the box, pushed it back in the cupboard, picked up the last letter her mother had written to Sam and took it downstairs.

She curled up in Sam's old recliner, wondering what had gone through his mind as he sat here. She wondered if he had missed her.

She shivered. Where was that afghan? She spotted it beside the end table. She was about to get it when she saw the Bible lying on the table. The Bible she'd once disdained because it had reminded her of Sam. A man she had always thought couldn't follow through on his Christian convictions.

A sob caught in her throat. Out of habit, she pushed it down. She hadn't shed any tears over Sam because she had thought he didn't deserve it.

How wrong she had been. How terribly, horribly wrong.

She put her head in her hands and sent out a heartfelt, simple prayer. "Lord, forgive me. I didn't know."

Then she opened the Bible and started reading, searching for comfort and for guidance.

"Glad you came to the picnic." Dodie laid her arm across Hannah's shoulder and gave her a one-armed hug. "And I'm really glad you came to church and I'm really glad the weather is cooperating."

Hannah smiled as she glanced up at the achingly blue sky stretched like a tent over the world. "It's gorgeous. I never see skies like this in Toronto."

"Of course not. This is sunny Alberta, rural style, and we don't have the smog and the humidity."

"Dodie, what lies are you propagating?" Ethan came toward them holding two plates piled high with a few salads, a huge slab of meat, some vegetables and topped with a bun that Hannah guessed was homemade, as well.

Dodie squeezed Hannah a little tighter, then whispered in her ear, "I'm glad you came. I haven't seen Ethan this happy in a long time."

She withdrew her arm and walked away, leaving Hannah blushing and confused yet curiously consoled about her decision to come today. After her discovery of the other night, she had thought of staying away.

Then Ethan had shown up at the house to pick her up. When he brushed a light kiss over her cheek, she thought she might find a way through all of this. So she got in the truck, sat beside him in church and was drawn into a service that comforted and strengthened her.

Ethan watched his cousin go, then turned to Hannah, handing her one of the plates. "Let's find a spot for us to sit."

She simply nodded, a curious warmth spreading through her at his use of the word *us*. As he held her gaze, his expression became more intense and his hand held hers tighter.

She felt it again. The curious connection that grew stronger each time they were together. She had thought she could keep things casual. Just be another girl on his list.

But they had shared much since she had come and she knew things were different between them.

And now, she had other information. She wasn't sure where to put her recent discovery but did know that, for today, she didn't want her discovery to intrude on her time with Ethan.

She followed him through the crowd of people, some of whom stopped them to chat. They finally found a place on the grass, in the lee of the church building.

"Now, this is what I call romantic," Ethan said with an ironic tone in his voice. "Right smack beside the graveyard."

"It's quiet," Hannah said, demurely sitting down a safe distance away. Her clothing options were limited so she had opted for a pair of dressier capris and a gauzy short-sleeved shirt over a camisole. Thankfully she didn't look out of place.

"Sorry I didn't think about a blanket or chairs," he said.

"I'm fine." Hannah started eating. Beyond them, children ran through the graveyard, appropriately carefree and full of life. Now and again one would bend over to read a stone, then hurry to catch up to their friends.

The living among the dead, she thought with a smile.

"Are your grandparents buried here?" Hannah asked, pointing with her fork at the graveyard.

"All my relatives are. Sam. My grandparents, great-grandparents and my aunt, my cousin, great-aunts and -uncles."

"Cousin?"

Ethan nodded. "Sarah's sister. Marilee. She died in a car accident a while back. She's buried beside her mother."

"So the Westerveld family has had its sadnesses, as well."

"No family is immune from hurt," Ethan said quietly, his eyes intent. "Like you. It must have been hard for you when your mother died."

"We weren't living together anymore. She was living in Saskatoon and I was back in Toronto."

"You two moved a lot, didn't you?"

She nodded. He probably knew. From Sam.

You should tell him what you found out, an insistent voice nagged from one corner of her mind.

Not yet. Not yet.

"Ethan. There you are. Dodie said you were coming." Dot bore down on them, her voice wide open and joyful. In her wake followed her husband, Morris. Hannah knew Dot from her sudden visit and Morris she'd seen in pictures Ethan had in the house.

Ethan got up as they came near and Hannah did the same.

Dot waved her hands at them. "Sit. Sit. We've eaten already, but we've been looking for you." She eased herself down on the chair her husband set out for her, then fanned herself with a paper plate that looked as if it had held dessert. Her sandy-blond hair, the same shade as Ethan's, was pulled up in a loose bun, her pink dress snug on her generous figure.

Morris set his own chair down and sat, as well. He gave Hannah a smile and leaned forward, his hands clasped between his knees. The sun shone off his balding head.

Hannah could see a bit of Sam in his cheekbones, the sparkle in his eyes and the dimple that appeared in one corner of his mouth when he smiled.

"So, what did you think of the service, Hannah?" Morris asked.

"Dad, for goodness' sake," Ethan protested.

"I enjoyed it a lot." Hannah ignored Ethan's huffing. And she had. The singing, the sermon, the Bible reading, had all called to the part of her that Sam had awoken with his prayers and his own Bible readings to her when she was younger. As she had listened to the service, she felt as if she could allow the old emotions she had experienced in church to come alive again.

She saw Morris's expression blossom and she sensed that he needed to know exactly why she had enjoyed it. She didn't mind expounding because to speak her thoughts aloud gave them shape and form. Morris and Dot seemed like people she could entrust with her fragile experience. "I especially liked the part the minister preached on. The passage about no longer being foreigners, but fellow citizens and members of God's household."

"An important message to be sure," Morris said, nodding as he spoke, his smile growing. "God uses family and household as a metaphor for the communion we receive in Him. Sam rediscovered that when he came here. I know he had moved away from his faith for a while."

Hannah couldn't stop the twinge of guilt she felt. Her mother had insisted on that when Sam moved in with them. And though Sam could have protested, his own faith was obviously not strong enough to fight the desire he had to be with her mother.

"…but we're thankful that God called him back," Morris continued. "And we're thankful he could see that family is a blessing that we have been given."

"Or a burden we have to bear," Ethan put in.

"I'm sure your burden is heavy indeed," Morris

said calmly, not even rising to Ethan's teasing. "How are you managing out here in the country, Hannah? Not too lonely?"

His concern was a two-edged sword. Hannah thought of Dodie's comment—that the family had wondered about her and what had happened to her.

And they had wondered in spite of the money Sam had sent to her mother.

She suppressed that thought. She reminded herself to deal with that later. Enjoy this moment.

"The quiet is doing me good and I'm enjoying the plants and my garden."

"You did a fantastic job with the flower gardens," Dot put in.

"And I hear you've been feeding Ethan's cows," Morris said. "You are a brave girl indeed."

"Running the tractor?" Dot asked, looking incredulous. "How did you manage that?"

"She's a natural, Mom. I showed her once how everything works and she caught on right away."

"And you coming from the city." Dot shook her head. "Guess you're a country girl at heart after all."

Her praise warmed Hannah's heart.

"Don't you guys move," a loud voice called out. "Janie and I are coming right away." Dodie waved from the lineup at the food table.

Ethan didn't seem pleased as Dodie, Janie and her kids plunked themselves down beside them and started chatting. But Hannah enjoyed the chatter, the conversation running ahead, turning and twisting, weaving through itself as it moved in no general direction.

Janie's children came and went. One of them took Hannah's plate; the other, Susie, brought her two desserts so she could pick. As if she could choose between homemade apple pie and blueberry cheesecake. Also homemade. So she ate both.

Somehow, in the process, Ethan ended up leaning on his elbow, bringing him closer to her.

Once he had reached up and brushed away a strand of her hair that had gotten caught against her lipstick. He had done it so casually his parents didn't seem to notice, but Hannah had seen Janie's eyes flick from Hannah to Ethan.

And she had smiled.

As the afternoon wore on Hannah discovered that Ethan was afraid of water, that Janie's husband had left her and their three children and was working up north on the rigs, that Sarah's father was recuperating from a stroke and Morris and Dot were going to be celebrating their thirty-fifth wedding anniversary in a couple of months.

Hannah was invited.

Family, she thought. This was what family was like.

An unexpected surge of anger pushed itself to the fore. How could her mother have kept this from her? How could her mother have assumed she had any right to the hard work Sam and Ethan had done on the farm?

Later. Later.

After some more conversation, some more jokes, Dodie got up, volunteering to do their share of the cleaning. Janie's kids started nagging at her. The afternoon was winding down.

"Guess we'd better be pushing off." Morris pressed his hands against his knees. "Mother, let me take your chair."

Slowly everyone else got up, said goodbye. As Janie and her children wandered off to the parking lot, Hannah and Ethan were finally alone. She watched the family leave and treasured the moment, tucking it away in a corner of her mind to pull out at another time and in another place.

Ethan gave her an apologetic look as he pulled her to her feet. "Sorry about that. My family tends to think that where two or more Westervelds are gathered, there should everyone else be."

"I didn't mind at all," Hannah said. "I like your family. They're pretty special people."

"And I think they like you." Ethan gave her a quick smile, then looked over his shoulder at the graveyard. "Do you want to visit Sam's grave?"

Sam's grave. She knew she should have stopped by the site sooner rather than later. Shame trembled through her as she realized that "later" had arrived.

"Thank you. I'd like to pay my respects to Sam."

They passed a number of older stones, some worn so much the names were barely legible, others tilting to one side as if weary of waiting for the resurrection that Sam had often talked about.

A stone didn't mark his grave yet, but the heaped, fresh dirt clearly showed his final resting place. A few faded flowers still lay on the dirt, and a plastic marker at the head of the grave held his name.

As she looked down at the grave, she didn't have to wonder if he missed her. He had.

Then, to her dismay, the cloud of doubt and shame she had been pushing aside all afternoon surrounded her, pulling away the defenses she had put up against it.

As a sob worked its way up her throat, tears trickled warmly down her cheek. She reached up and surreptitiously wiped away one tear, then another.

"I know how you feel," he said quietly, putting his arm around her and pulling her close. "I miss him so much sometimes."

She looked up at him and finally dared to voice the thoughts she had kept to herself until now. "I found the papers."

"Papers?"

"Bank statements. He'd been sending money to my mom all along." Her voice wavered but she had started and she wanted to finish. Standing here, in front of Sam's grave, she wanted to honor what he had done. "I never knew, but all those years he'd been supporting us."

"I know." Ethan brushed a strand of hair away from her face and tucked it gently behind her ear. "But it doesn't matter anymore," he said.

"But it does." Her throat thickened and she swallowed. And swallowed. She had to finish this. "I always thought that I didn't matter to him, that he had walked away and forgot about me, but he didn't. I never knew, Ethan. I never knew." She turned to him, clinging to his shoulders, determined to make him believe her. "I always thought the money we lived on was welfare money...." Her voice broke.

Ethan cupped her cheek and smiled gently down on her. "I was wondering about that."

"I never even said goodbye to him," she whispered. "The last time I saw him, he was standing by his car, looking up at me. I should have run down and begged him to stay. But I let my mother pull me away. My mother kept me from Sam, from the only father I ever knew. And she did it for so many years. How could she have done that to me?" She sniffed and Ethan's arm tightened. Then his other arm came around her and she was pressed against him.

Sorrow blossomed in her chest, and in this safe haven she couldn't hold back or be strong.

She began to weep, her sorrow flowing over her like a tidal wave, pulling her loose from the moorings of her rigid self-control. She gave in, letting Ethan hold her as she wept, as her body, racked with sobs, shook and trembled.

Her tears flowed for Sam, for her mother, for the mess of her life.

And all the while, Ethan held her, stroking her hair, murmuring quiet words of encouragement and sympathy. She leaned against him, thankful for his strength and support as sorrow, long suppressed, found a safe outlet.

Finally, the storm subsided and she leaned against Ethan, his shirt damp beneath her cheek from her tears. She sniffed once more, reaching up to wipe her nose with the tissue that had somehow appeared in her hands. Ethan, she suspected. She should pull away but was loath to leave the haven of his arms.

"I'm sorry, Hannah," Ethan whispered, his hand cupping her head. "I'm so sorry for all you've had to deal with."

She closed her eyes as his deep voice soothed the pain in her heart.

He was a good man, she thought. She had been foolish to think she could engage in a simple flirtation with him.

With a gentle movement, she drew back, but Ethan didn't let go of her. He looked down on her and she caught the flicker of an emotion that shook her to her core.

He cares about me.

And on the heels of that thought came one even more frightening.

I care about him.

Before she could formulate any kind of coherent protest, Ethan lowered his head and kissed her. His kiss was tender yet with a hint of deeper emotion.

Hannah returned his kiss and clung to him.

Then as Ethan drew away, as his rough, callused fingers, the fingers of a man who worked the land, trailed gently down her cheek, she reached up and cupped his face in her hand.

"You're special to me," he said quietly.

Those few words, devastating in their simplicity, dived into her heart.

She couldn't form a reply. Her moments with Ethan had been, in her mind, like a time out of time. Something she could indulge in to ease her loneliness.

But his presence and these moments had slowly permeated all areas of her life and mind. He had become important to her, his presence something she had come to expect and look forward to. The barriers she had thought would keep him away from the rest of her life had been eased away by time and proximity and shared experiences.

As she realized what he had come to mean to her, a flicker of hope whispered within her. Maybe she could stay, maybe she didn't have to leave.

She turned gently back into Ethan's arms, letting the whisper gain strength and voice.

Maybe. Just maybe.

Dear Lord, she prayed, *help me make the right decision. Show me what I should do.*

Chapter Fifteen

"You're not going to change my mind on this, Jace." Ethan looked out the dining room window of the house. Hannah was pulling weeds in the flower garden and didn't know he was inside. "I'm not going through with it." Ethan watched Hannah move a little farther away, Scout following her. "Thanks for being a good lawyer. Now be a friend and let it go. No, nothing has happened yet...of course I have hopes, but I'm realistic, too. I'm not going chasing after any woman no matter what...we'll see what happens. Goodbye, Jace."

Ethan disconnected the call as second thoughts assailed his confidence. The farm had always been his life. Dodie had, on occasion, accused him of making it his idol. So had Colby.

The thought of his ex-fiancée pricked his conscience. He had put off returning her call. He had moved so far from their previous relationship that they had nothing in common except a few memories that he preferred to keep buried.

He shifted his stance so he could see out the window without being seen. All he saw of Hannah was her profile as she worked. A smile softened her features.

After Sunday, when she had cried in his arms, when he had comforted her in their shared sorrow, he had felt as if the focus of his life had shifted a quarter turn. It still disoriented him to realize how fully she had become integrated into his life. He had gotten used to coming back onto the yard and seeing her working in the garden, mowing the lawn, feeding the chickens.

The feelings that she arose in him were different than any he had felt before. And they frightened him.

She hadn't said she wasn't leaving. She hadn't given him any indication of her plans.

So he had stayed away, hoping that distance might change the suddenly changing feelings she brought out in him.

Then yesterday he had come out of the shop and seen her nailing a loose board on a fence. He had to physically restrain himself from going over to help her, laugh with her.

She didn't have to help with the chores. She could have sat in the house all day and at the end she still would have been entitled to half of the farm. Instead she helped and he saw her pleasure in the work, the look on her face when she saw the calves being born, the smile of satisfaction she flashed him when she drove the tractor.

This morning, he realized he was fighting a losing battle with his emotions. After much thought and prayer, he had made a critical decision concerning the farm. He had to let it go. He had to stop looking so far into the future and worrying about what might come.

In spite of the money he had put into the farm, he also realized he was only a steward of what had been given him. And as a good steward, he had to let go of what he thought was all his and, without any opposition from him, let Hannah decide what to do with what was hers.

Hannah, the woman he loved.

The words gently entered his mind.

He loved her.

And what surprised him the most—the thought didn't send him into an initial flurry of backpedaling as it had with Colby.

That had been an entirely different situation, he realized, looking at his former relationship through the eyes of this one.

Hannah created deeper emotions in him. He wanted to give her whatever he could. He wanted to let go of control and be there for her.

Please, Lord, help me to care for her the way I should. To want what is best for her always in spite of what she decides.

His prayer rose out of a heart full of thanks and love.

The day suddenly held more light, more air, more of everything. He wanted to rush out and tell her now. Yet something, a still voice, cautioned him to wait.

He had time. The last thing he wanted to do was spook her with a heartfelt declaration she might not be ready for. He was still unsure of where he stood with her, only that he felt a connection he knew couldn't be one-sided. He knew, in his heart, she felt something, too.

He had time. He had to go to town to pick up some ear tags for the cows before he put them out on pasture and, after that, no plans.

But he had one other phone call to make.

Two days now.

Two days, and seven hours since the last time Ethan had kissed her, Hannah thought as she swept up the last bits of dirt from the paving stones of the backyard. And two days since she had seen him last.

Four days and thirteen hours since you told him about Colby.

Was that why he was staying away?

But he had kissed her since that call. Had taken

her to church and the church barbecue and had comforted her at her most vulnerable moment.

Maybe he regretted that move. Maybe he's got cold feet.

She pushed the last bit of dirt off the stones, wishing she could as easily sweep away the thoughts running through her mind. She had prayed about her and Ethan, just as the minister had suggested. Just as she had read in the Bible. She walked into the house and, out of habit, checked for messages. But nothing from any of the girls who had once filled up the machine, nothing from Ethan.

Cast all your cares on him...

If Ethan wanted to keep his distance and if he was regretting what had happened the past few days, then she had to accept that.

Cast all your cares on him...

The sound of a vehicle broke into her thoughts and the sound made Hannah's heart flip again.

Ethan?

No. This was a quieter vehicle. Like a car.

Hannah walked to the window, hoping, praying it wasn't Dodie or Dot or a salesman. She couldn't face anyone right now.

The door opened and a young woman got out of the car. She wore her blond hair up in a twist and, as she walked around the car, Hannah could see that she was petite, slim and stunningly beautiful.

She opened the door on the other side and

helped a little girl with short blond curls out of the car. The woman picked the girl up and carried her to the house.

More relatives. Would she ever meet them all? Hannah wondered, pushing her own unruly and dusty hair back from her face. She noticed the twin circles of dirt staining her green cotton capris and the bits of leaves and grass still clinging to her faded brown T-shirt.

Oh well.

She walked to the door and opened it just as the woman stepped onto the deck.

"Hello, there," Hannah said, forcing a smile to her face. Though her emotions were a turmoil of plans and thoughts and regrets, she was determined to be polite and welcoming.

The woman looked exhausted and the little girl drooped against her mother as the woman turned to Hannah.

"Are you Hannah?"

"Yes."

She gave Hannah a weary smile and brushed a loose strand of hair back from her face. "Sorry to barge in on you like this, but I need to see Ethan. Is he here?"

"Sorry. I don't know where he is. May I ask who you are?"

"But…doesn't he live here?" She frowned as she ignored Hannah's question.

Hannah shook her head. "He lives in a holiday trailer, close to the barns."

"I see," the woman said, a more hopeful note in her voice. "I'm Ethan's old fiancée, Colby. This is Esther, our little girl."

Our.

As the woman casually dropped this bomb into Hannah's life, the little girl laid her head on the woman's shoulder and stared back at Hannah with bleary, gray-green eyes.

Eyes the color of sage.

Full circle, Hannah thought. Her life had come around to her own beginning. A woman with a young girl, alone and seeking help from a Westerveld. Only in this case, the Westerveld was the biological father.

Every ounce of fight she had left her like the air out of a balloon.

"Come in, please," Hannah said, holding the door open for them, clinging to it like a life preserver. "You must be tired."

"Yes, very. Since Ethan called me, I've been driving all night." Colby walked into the house and looked around, a bemused expression on her face. "I forgot how nice this house was." Her tone was wistful and as she looked around the kitchen and into the living room, Hannah resisted the urge to straighten, neaten and tidy.

But more important, she had to fight the

feelings of resentment that crowded her throat. Once upon a time this was going to be Colby's. And she had come back because Ethan had called her. Was this why he had stayed away?

Hannah released her grip on the door.

"Sit down, I'll get you something to eat and drink," she said to Colby, surprised that the weakness in her legs and the wobble in her heart didn't come out in her voice.

"Thanks. That would be nice." Colby picked up the little girl and sat down, holding her on her lap.

Hannah poured the iced tea she had made for Ethan and put out the cookies from the church picnic while she gathered her thoughts, disjointed and uprooted by Colby's unexpected appearance.

"I'm curious—why are you living in the house and Ethan in the trailer?" Colby asked.

Hannah tried to give Colby her complete attention. "I'm here for a while."

"How so?"

"Sam willed half of the farm to me."

"Half of the farm? How did that… What was he… How? Who are you?"

Hannah understood her shock and surprise, but the question Colby tacked on at the end raised her hackles. And now that she had actually seen hackles on the chickens, she knew better what that expression truly meant.

She put the plate and the glasses on the table, a

small plastic one for Esther, a larger glass one for Colby, and sat across from the mother and her child, trying to find a way to explain a situation that she had become uncomfortable with herself.

"Sam lived with my mother and me for a number of years. Then when his father got hurt, he came back to the farm. My mother and I never saw him again. I think he willed me half of the farm because he was trying to make up for being a part of our lives and then being gone."

But even as she mentally recited the lines that had sustained her claim since she came here, she lost her conviction. Sam had more than paid any debt, real or imagined, to her and her mother.

"But Ethan has poured his heart and soul into this farm. He has made so many sacrifices, has put so much money into it, for him to have to share that…"

Colby's voice drifted off, but her words echoed in the kitchen, harshly underlining Hannah's own uncertainty.

"I'm thirsty, Mommy." Esther's plaintive voice drew her attention and, with a gentle smile, Colby lifted the cup to her daughter's mouth, helping her along.

Hannah watched, unable to keep her eyes off the little girl with the unusual eyes. "How old is she?"

Colby shot her a look from beneath a strand of hair that had slipped out of her bun and into her eyes. "Three years old."

Three years ago, according to Dodie, Colby had walked away from Ethan. Was it because of this child?

"I made the biggest mistake of my life when I called off the wedding," Colby said. She drew in a shuddering breath but continued. "I was so afraid of what my parents would say when they found out I was pregnant. What Ethan's parents would say. I was so ashamed." She pressed her lips together then pulled out a handkerchief from her pocket and wiped her eyes. She glanced down at Esther and a smile trembled on her lips. "I love my little girl and I'm never sorry about her. But I should have thought of her instead of myself when I called the wedding off."

Each word she spoke twisted the knife that had lodged itself in Hannah's breastbone. She clutched her own glass, trying to absorb what Colby was saying. Ethan had a little girl.

And behind that came another chilling thought. Ethan had been intimate with this woman.

"When I called and you answered the phone, I thought I was too late," Colby whispered, dabbing at her eyes again. "I thought he had found someone to take my place." She blinked, her blue eyes large in her pale face, her expression entreating Hannah. "But he hasn't, has he?"

And what was she supposed to say to that?

Ethan had told her she was special and then he had stayed away.

"I still love him and I want to make a home for me and my little girl. I want us to be a family," Colby continued, not waiting for Hannah's reply.

"He is such a good man. I know he'll do what's right."

With each word that fell from Colby's perfect lips, Hannah felt the ground she had thought was firm beneath her shift and change. She had no firm foundation.

This farm wasn't hers and Ethan wasn't hers.

You don't belong here, the voice said. *You need to leave and let go.*

No. She was going to fight. Ethan said... Ethan said...

Ethan said nothing more than that you are special.

But she knew there was something deeper, lasting between them.

"Mommy, where's Daddy?" Esther asked, her small voice piercing Hannah's heart.

Hannah pushed herself away from the table, trying to find her bearings. She walked to the counter, looked out the window, her hands clenching the counter to find stability. The chickens were scratching in the yard, some dusting themselves in the loose dirt by a wooden granary. Beyond the fences she could see the cows grazing in the pasture, a hawk circling lazily above them.

Peace reigned here. Ethan belonged here.

She didn't.

Her heart floundered even as common sense fought with anger. How could Ethan have kept a daughter from her? How could he have thought she might not want to know this?

But what was she supposed to do?

"I can see my daughter and I have taken up enough of your time. I'd better be going. Tell Ethan I'm at my parents' place."

Hannah couldn't look back as she heard Colby's chair scrape back over the floor, the sound cutting like a knife. "C'mon, honey, we're going to Grandma and Grandpa's place."

"Wanna stay here," Esther said. "I don't want to go."

Hannah closed her eyes, Esther's complaint drawing out a memory that Hannah thought she had buried. She and her mother, getting ready to leave yet another apartment. And then, in the Laundromat, while they were washing the clothes they had packed, they had met Sam.

And Hannah's life had suddenly become one of light and laughter.

"Thanks for the drink," Colby said quietly. Hannah heard her get up. Then the door shut behind her and a few moments later Hannah watched as Colby buckled her daughter in her car seat, got in the car and drove slowly off the yard.

As the shock of the news wore off, Hannah's anger blossomed and she felt like hitting something, someone. She wanted to scream, to cry.

She wanted to hit Ethan.

She thought she was special to Ethan. She thought she mattered enough to know what had happened in Ethan's life. But, as the dust of Colby's car settled onto the yard, Hannah felt a harder truth grab hold of her.

She had no right to be here. Sam had already done more than was expected for a daughter that wasn't his. Sam had done what her natural father should have done—supported and cared for her.

Hannah swayed as she bowed her head, anger and sorrow storming through her. Why had Ethan held this back from her?

And what right did you have to know?

He had kissed her, told her she was special. She had thought they were moving toward something deeper. Something lasting.

How could they build on a foundation of mistrust?

But below her anger and frustration lay a deeper struggle between her feelings for Ethan and an ingrained sense of justice when she discovered how much money her mother had already taken from Sam. Could Hannah think she had a right to any part of the farm now?

But Sam wanted to give it to you. Because he felt guilty about leaving you.

Thoughts of Sam sent her mind scurrying back into her own past. How much fuller would her life be if Sam had stayed with her and her mother?

Ethan, more than Sam, had an obligation to be a father to this little girl, a husband to the woman who bore her.

And where did Hannah fit into this scenario?

Her heart grew still and cold in her chest.

She didn't. She couldn't.

She cared too much for Ethan to be a spectator of this relationship. It would hurt too much to watch him with his daughter and Colby, knowing that she could never be a part of his life anymore.

She closed her eyes, tears of bitterness and disappointment flowing down her cheeks. *Help me, Lord,* she prayed. *Help me make the right decision.*

The thrum of the bus's tires on the frost heaves beat like angry fists against Hannah's head. She laid her head against the cool window of the Greyhound bus, trying to cool her heated cheeks. Fields of undulating green flowed past her hazy reflection. The trees were in full leaf, and in the pastures cows lay contented in the lush grass.

Looked like it was going to be a good year after all.

Hannah closed her eyes against the low-level headache that had started when she saw Colby and Ethan's little girl and had stayed while she packed her clothes and said goodbye to Scout.

As she walked away from the house, she'd hesitated by Ethan's trailer, wondering whether she should write a note.

And what would you have put on there? she thought bitterly.

Good luck with the secret daughter? Sorry that you messed up all those years ago? Sorry that you have a responsibility to take care of? Sorry that you're exactly the man you always claimed you weren't?

She didn't owe Ethan anything. Not even an explanation. Her first impression of Ethan had been right all along. And she had been suckered.

The angry thoughts had spun and twisted through her head, but they fought with reality and with the memories she had. Ethan claiming he never invited the attention he got. Ethan not answering the phone calls. Ethan telling her how much she mattered to him.

And yet…

Hannah knew what it was like to live without a father. Ethan had to do the right thing and, in spite of how she felt, Hannah wasn't going to stand in the way of that happening.

Should she have talked to Ethan first?

She closed her eyes against the other voice, listing for herself all the reasons she had to leave.

Hannah had no right to be on the farm anyhow, not after finding out about the money.

Esther needed her father.

Ethan didn't deserve her time.

Forgive me, Lord, she prayed, trying to find some solace in her newfound relationship with God. *Help me stop thinking of myself and think of what's best for Esther, Colby and Ethan.*

She laid her head against the seat, but sleep wouldn't come. How was she going to manage all the way back to Toronto? And what was she going to do when she got there?

The miles and the questions slipped by and, half an hour after leaving Riverbend, the bus pulled into Preston. A few people got off, some more got on.

A red truck pulled into the parking lot of the store the bus used as a depot and Hannah's heart jumped. A bright red truck that looked exactly like Ethan's.

She shook off the silly notion as she closed her eyes again. She didn't know where Ethan was and he certainly wouldn't know where she was. She had hitchhiked from the farm, and thankfully had gotten a ride within five minutes of heading out.

"I'm sorry, mister, you need a ticket," the driver was saying to someone who was trying to get on the bus.

"I just need a minute with one of your passengers."

Hannah's eyes flew open. Was that Ethan's voice?

"You can talk, but from outside and you only got half a minute," the driver growled. "I'm behind schedule as it is."

"Hannah, if you can hear me, I need to talk to you. I can explain everything." The voice carried to the back of the bus and Hannah's heart jumped.

She pressed her head against the window and, sure enough, there stood Ethan, one foot on the step, his hands braced against the door frame as he called into the bus.

She closed her eyes, wishing he would leave. *Go back to your daughter,* she mentally urged him. *Go take care of your responsibilities. I'm not a part of your life anymore.*

"Sorry. Guess she's not on this bus," the driver said. The doors swung shut and Ethan stepped back a few steps, his eyes scanning the windows.

He can't see you, Hannah reminded herself as she drew back.

The bus pulled away and Hannah relaxed against the seat. But as they turned out of town and the vehicle gained speed, her eyes thickened with unshed tears.

It was over, she reminded herself. It had been a lovely dream but reality has taken hold once again. She didn't deserve to be there and Ethan had other obligations.

She closed her eyes and tumbled into a fitful sleep.

When the bus pulled into yet another small town, she woke again. She stretched and got up, her neck kinked from lying at an unnatural angle.

She heard some murmuring from passengers at the front of the bus and saw a few people leaning closer to the window. Curious, she glanced over herself.

A bright red truck had pulled into the lot right beside the bus.

And Ethan got out.

Hannah pressed her hand against her suddenly frantic heart as she dropped back in her seat. What was he doing? Why was he following her? Why wasn't he back in Riverbend? Why wasn't he with Colby and Esther?

"You're one persistent person," the driver said with a laugh as he got off the bus. "But you still can't go on without a ticket."

"That's okay. Don't need a ticket to yell."

The rumble of Ethan's voice, muffled by the seats in front of her, set her heart pounding even harder.

"Hannah, I know you're on this bus," he called out, doing exactly as he had said he would. "And I'm not going to quit following you until you come off and talk to me, so if you don't want me to waste a ton of gas chasing you all the way back to Toronto, you may as well come off now."

Passengers looked around expectantly, as if trying to identify Ethan's prey. Hannah's cheeks grew warm as she tried to think.

"C'mon, Hannah, give the guy a break," one voice called out.

"He looks like he's pretty serious, Hannah," another voice said.

"Hannah, Hannah," two young girls started chanting. And soon the rest of the passengers joined in.

Her cheeks were flaming as Hannah got to her feet and slung her purse over her shoulder. Might as well get this over and done with.

"He's a honey, Hannah," the one girl called out. "If you don't want him, let me have a chance."

Hannah kept her face down as she walked down the aisle of the bus and then, as she stepped from the bus, there he was, his hair backlit by the sun, his cheeks unshaved, his shirt wrinkled.

"Hey, there," he said quietly, as she came to stand in front of him. "Where are you going?"

She swallowed the thickness that threatened to close off her throat. "I was going back to Toronto. Where I belong."

Ethan's expression fell. "But if you leave, you won't get your half of the farm."

She fiddled with the strap of her purse, unable

to meet his eyes. Those gentle, gray-green eyes, the color of sage. "I never had any right to the farm. Not after I found those statements."

"Sam wanted you to have half. You didn't take off because of that?"

She shook her head. "Colby stopped by the farm—"

"Colby?" The name came out as a bark. "She came to the farm?"

"This morning. With your daughter, Esther."

Ethan's puzzled expression could not be faked. "I don't have a daughter."

Hannah wanted so badly to believe him, but she couldn't ignore what Colby had told her. "But Colby said that Esther—"

Ethan plowed his hand through his hair. "If she told you that, she's lying. We were never, ever, intimate."

He spoke with such conviction. Hannah read sincerity in the steadiness of his sage-green eyes. She swallowed and felt the rage she'd clung to as a defense against him slowly dissipate.

"But why would she say that?" Her voice was quiet, hardly daring to voice the doubts that had beat against her anger.

"Because she's Colby. Because I made a big mistake when I phoned her to tell her to stay out of my life. I told her what you meant to me. That she had never meant the same. I didn't suspect that she would come to the farm and try to jeopardize that." He lifted his hands but only touched Hannah on her cheek. "I may have had a lot of girlfriends, but I don't have any children anywhere. I hope you believe that I'm not that kind of guy."

Relief sluiced through her, followed by shame that she had thought exactly that. But behind that came a profound sense of thankfulness. And love. "I believe you."

He nodded. "It wasn't until Colby called me that I realized what you meant to me. I was hoping to take you out on a romantic picnic and do it all right, but when I came to the house, you were gone. You didn't even leave me a note. I had to guess what was happening." He shook his head, his hand resting lightly on her shoulder. "I caught a break when I got to town and Pearl told me that she saw you get on the bus. I owe her, big-time."

"What do you mean?" Hannah was trying to keep up with the information Ethan poured out.

"About what?"

"What I mean to you?"

A person trying to get on the bus jostled her and Ethan drew her aside, his hands holding her arms, his fingers lightly caressing her skin as he looked deeply into her eyes.

"When I came to the house and you were gone, I got scared. More scared than when I got the news at the rehearsal from Colby's dad. More scared than when I found out that Sam had willed half of the farm away." He leaned closer, his voice lowering, sending shivers dancing down her spine. "Hannah, I love you. I love you more than I've ever loved anyone before. I love you enough to step aside and let you decide what you want to do with your half of the farm. I'm willing to let it go, but I'm hoping I won't have to. I'm hoping you'll stay—and stay with me. I'm hoping… I'm hoping that what I thought was happening between us isn't a figment of my imagination. I'm hoping that I'm right and that you'll marry me."

Hannah could only stare as her tired, frantic mind tried to absorb the reality of what he was saying. Ethan was asking her to marry him?

She breathed in, holding the moment as if too much movement, too many words, would break it. This handsome, loving, kind man with gray-green eyes and unruly blond hair was asking her to marry him?

She closed her eyes, drawing out the moment, savoring it. She took a long, slow breath, opened her eyes and smiled at this man who was giving her so much she doubted he even knew the enormity of his gift.

"Yes, Ethan. I'll marry you."

His shoulders sagged and he leaned his forehead against hers, his features blurring.

"Thank you, Hannah Kristoferson," he whispered.

"So, kiss him already," a voice called out from inside the bus.

Ethan drew back, gave her a crooked smile, then dragged her into his arms, his exuberant kiss sealing the deal.

As Hannah wrapped her arms around his neck, anchoring her claim on him, a chorus of cheers arose from the bus. Ethan drew back, tossed off a salute, then drew Hannah away.

"C'mon. Let's go home."

"But my bag—"

"Is right here." The bus driver handed Ethan the ratty knapsack and he slung it over one shoulder, slipping his other arm around her shoulder. "Can we go now?"

Hannah nodded. Ethan dropped another kiss on her lips, then escorted her back to the truck and drove her back home. Back to the farm, to friends and to family.

* * * * *

Dear Reader,

I wrote this book because I know of situations where men have lived with women who have children and when the relationship is over, even though each may have very legitimate reasons for breaking it off, it's the children who are hurt the most.

I'm sure there are many children who are the unwilling victims of such breakups. I wanted to write this book from the viewpoint of one of the children who was left behind. And I wanted to give this girl a happy ending.

I know there are many lost and hurting souls out there. My prayer for you is that you may find your family and your security in the love of a Father whose love is perfect and pure.

Carolyne Aarsen

QUESTIONS FOR DISCUSSION

1. What is your opinion of Sam's will? How would you have reacted?

2. Some members of the Westerveld family struggled with accepting the situation in Sam's past. Are there people in your family who aren't living right whom you have to deal with? What do you think is the right response?

3. Do you think Ethan was justified in his reaction to the will? Why or why not?

4. In your opinion, what were some of the less obvious reasons Hannah spent so much time fixing up the yard? Were all of them justified?

5. What is your opinion of Ethan's actions concerning other women? Why do you think he acted that way?

6. If you met someone like Hannah's mother, how do you think you would treat her?

7. How would you react if you had overheard Ethan's comment about Hannah being a freeloader? Was he justified in saying this?

8. The book ends with Ethan chasing after Hannah. What was it about her that made him humble himself like that?

9. Did you think Hannah was justified in agreeing to the terms of the will? Why or why not?

10. What do you think Sam was trying to accomplish by putting the conditions he did on the will?

11. If you lived in a city or town and had to move to a farm, what would be some of the adjustments you would have to make?

12. What was the significance of Sam's garden to Hannah?

SUSPENSE

RIVETING INSPIRATIONAL ROMANCE

Watch for our new series of
edge-of-your-seat suspense novels.
These contemporary tales
of intrigue and romance
feature Christian characters
facing challenges to their faith...
and their lives!

**Steeple
Hill®**

Visit:
www.SteepleHill.com